Coffee Boys

Rose Blackwell

Published by Rose Blackwell, 2024.

COFFEE BOYS

First edition. March 31, 2024.

ISBN: 979-8224655984

Written by Rose Blackwell.

Table of Contents

To the real life Dominic. Thank you for providing safe space.

Chapter One: A Shot of Caramel

Coffee Boys had always been one of Seattle's trendiest cafes, but it didn't reach its current level of fame until Betty Blond, a local food blogger, wrote a comedic post about it for an online lifestyle magazine called *Daffodils*. She described our caramel-fudge macchiato as "an orgasmic experience of nipple-hardening whipped cream and chocolate that will titillate both the tastebuds and the imagination." Klyde thought the whole review was hilarious; he printed it off, put it in a fancy frame, and hung it on the wall behind the register. I wasn't complaining either. It was a weird way to describe an innocent cup of coffee, but it brought a lot of new customers to the café and my hours doubled.

I had worked at Coffee Boys for about six months before Betty wrote her article. Shockingly, this wasn't my initial life plan. I went to college with dreams of becoming a botanist because bright-eyed, eighteen-year-old Theodore Brooks saw nothing problematic about sinking thousands of dollars into pursuing a career dedicated to flowers and dirt. I had trouble finding work in my field and eventually I had to consider the possibility that I had made a poor life decision. So I quit my job working in the garden section at Lowe's, and while I was in the process of having an existential crisis, Klyde took pity on me. I used to go to Coffee Boys a lot when I was a student and during that time, we became pretty good friends. So he was more than willing to give me a job while I figured my shit out.

Klyde's full name was Klaus-Leonardo Vincent DePaul. He was a beanpole with a scraggly beard and thick brown hair that he insisted on wearing in a man bun. I told him it made him look like a douche, but the only thing I got for this fair criticism was the finger. Questionable hairstyles aside, Klyde was a pretty good guy. When he found out I was gay, the first thing he asked me was what I thought of his shoes— a bit stereotypical, but hardly the worst reaction I'd ever received.

There are only a few days in my life that I remember with absolute clarity.

July 18th, 12:00 P.M., out in the garden with Dad and learning about the flowers that sparked my initial interest in botany. I still dreamed about the red lilies that bloomed near the fence. They were like a streak of fire in the grass.

September 9th, 10:01 A.M., in the hallway just after calculus. My first kiss was with a junior named Rick Seymour. It was wet and wholly unremarkable. But he smelled nice. Like citrus and clean linen.

August 24th, 12:32 P.M., a gym auditorium, the rain outside pounding a fierce staccato rhythm on the windowpanes. The day I got my B.A.

And finally, October 18th, 11:34 A.M, inside Coffee Boys on a bright, cold day when the trees outside the big front window were heavy with caps of burning gold and copper. The morning I met Dominic.

The day started out as a dumpster fire.

I can usually tell within ten seconds of meeting a person if they will be dead to me. I always introduce myself as Theodore, and if they come back with a chipper, "Nice to meet you, Theo," I don't waste time getting to know them. I don't know why people think it's socially acceptable to switch my name without my permission, but these are the same morons who will send their coffee back because you put one too many ice cubes into their iced mocha. Now imagine having a room full of such people. Then imagine banging your head repeatedly against the wall. That's the kind of morning I was having on October 18th.

"What can I get you?" I asked the two women sitting in a booth near the counter.

"Hello there," said the one on the right, giving me a smile that belonged in a Colgate commercial. She had red braids and too many freckles. She squinted at my nametag, which clearly read "Theodore." Then she tossed her head and continued brightly: "We'll have a couple of black coffees, Theo. No cream or sugar."

You can have my foot up your ass, lady.

"Sure thing, miss. I'll put that in for you right away."

I went and fetched their coffee, resisting the urge to fart in their mugs. When I set them down on the table, the redhead's friend—a woman with giant blonde curls—grimaced and said:

"Could you bring me some milk whenever you get a chance?"

"Oh, they don't have any on the table?" the redhead asked, frowning at her friend's cup and then at me.

No, you shit stain. I did not bring you the fucking milk because you didn't say you wanted fucking milk.

"Oh, I'm sorry, miss. I'll grab that for you right away."

"Thanks, Theo!"

"You're a doll."

You both deserve to be flung headfirst into a wall.

The old man I served after them wasn't much better.

"Hey—Theo, right?"

No, you fucking mouth breather.

"Yessir, what is it?"

"Are refills free?"

"They're eighty-three cents."

"But all I want is coffee."

No, really? You came into a coffee shop for coffee? Get the fuck out of town.

"Well, yes, but all refills are eighty-three cents, sir..."

"What if I don't get whipped cream this time?"

Am I fucking stuttering? Jesus Horatio Christ!

"It will still be eighty-three cents, sir."

"Well, fine, I guess...throw in a little vanilla too if you can."

I went to the counter to refill the guy's order, taking several deep breaths on the way there. I squirted a flavor shot into the coffee and only noticed after I put the bottle down that the sticky residue on the plastic had transferred to my hands.

Fantastic. Just ducky.

I turned and washed my hands in the sink, scrubbing until the skin on my knuckles started flaking and my palms turned raw pink—-twenty-one seconds, to be exact, not because I had any particular affinity for the number, but because that's just how long it took for my hands to feel clean. Then I went and took the old fart his stupid vanilla coffee, making a mental note to wipe down all the flavor bottles before the end of my shift.

"Hey, would you take care of the guy who just walked in?" Klyde asked, looking up from the register as I walked by with a tray of empty mugs. "I need to whip up some other orders real quick."

"Sure. I guess I haven't fucking suffered enough today."

"Poor baby. Why don't you write a poem about it later, and do your job now?"

"Why don't you take that whipped cream nozzle and—" I couldn't finish the thought because a couple of college girls wandered up to the counter. Klyde turned towards them with an obsequious smile and said in a sing-song voice:

"Well hello, ladies. What can I get for you on this fine day?"

I gave him a filthy look as I snatched up a pen and paper pad and strode over to the man sitting by the window. My first thought was that he looked like a college professor. He was tall, broad-shouldered, and slender, but not skinny. Under his gray blazer was a snug black turtleneck, and I could see the muscular curves of a well-toned chest. He was wearing matching gray trousers and gleaming black shoes that looked like they cost more than my rent. Maybe not a college professor then. A corporate stooge? Yeah, he definitely looked like he could be a douche with a corner office and a drawer full of fancy ties.

"Welcome to Coffee Boys. What can I get you?" I asked dully.

He'd been staring out the window, but he turned towards me with a little start, like he'd forgotten he was in a public area and other people might talk at some point. He was wearing square, black-rimmed glasses, and his dark, windswept hair tumbled over his forehead and the tips of his ears. He absently ran a hand through it as he looked up at me—which only made it stick up more.

"Could I get a small coffee with two creams? No sugar."

"Sure. Any flavor shots?"

He paused. His eyes wandered over my face, like he was committing it to memory—or deciding whether or not he was going to punch it. It was hard to tell. He had an expression on his face that I couldn't decipher.

Is this guy high?

Then the stranger smiled. He had lips like rosebuds. My gaze lingered on them for a fraction of a second longer than was socially appropriate.

"Caramel would be nice," he said.

"How many?"

"Just one."

"You got it."

I turned and went to the counter to make up his order. When I went back to his table, he didn't seem as absent-minded as before. He was looking at me now with an almost predatory intensity.

Does he expect me to break into song or something?

I carefully set a steaming mug in front of him.

"Here you go, sir. Enjoy."

"Thanks. And I'm terribly sorry to bother you again—"

Here it comes. Did I forget something you didn't order in the first place? I swear to God.

"Could I also get a slice of strawberry cheesecake too?"

"Oh—yeah, sure. I'm pretty sure we have some left."

"Thanks a bunch."

He's definitely high.

I went over to the counter once more, bent down, and checked out the treats we had in the display case.

"Hey, is that guy bothering you?" Klyde muttered out of the corner of his mouth as he squatted next to me and selected a big brownie. "He looks intense."

"I think he's on something," I hissed between my teeth. "Don't make eye contact."

"Just don't get into a car with him, alright?"

"Oh, gee, do you think that would be a bad idea, Dad?" I said mockingly, straightening up with a plate of strawberry cheesecake in my hand.

"At least he's got good taste," Klyde said, puffing out his chest as he looked proudly at the slice of cake. He came in early to make it from scratch every morning. Personally, I couldn't see why people liked it so much. It looked like something sneezed out by a cat.

"Or no taste buds at all," I said, turning around and walking off. I heard Klyde mutter something under his breath that sounded a lot like "little shit."

"Thank you, Theodore," the guy said when I slid the cake next to his coffee mug.

Alright, points for you, freak, you can read.

"Sure thing. Can I get you anything else?"

He hesitated and gave me another strange stare. Then he shook his head.

"I'm all set."

I walked off to deal with the group of college kids who had just wandered into the café. I glanced over at the professor a couple times as I bustled about the floor. He seemed very focused on that cheesecake—and when I say focused, I mean I actually witnessed him shoot a furtive gaze around the room before he raised the plate to his lips and give it a quick lick, lapping up the last of the strawberry drizzle.

"I can take that for you," I said as I passed by a few minutes later. He'd been sitting there for about thirty minutes now. I had a tray in my hands and was going around collecting cups from empty tables.

"Oh—sure, thanks."

"Or I could stand here and block you from view if you want to get a bit more of that strawberry sauce."

He stared at me for a moment, then laughed. An embarrassed flush crept into his cheeks. He looked oddly boyish for a second.

"And here I was thinking I'd gotten away with it."

"You might've if you weren't, you know, in public."

As I gathered up his mug, I glanced inside and noticed a thick layer of caramel syrup congealed on the bottom. I held it up with a wry smile.

"Is it okay if I take this, or did you want a final moment with the caramel sauce too?"

He laughed again and shook his head. "Go ahead. I don't really like it anyway. I just said caramel because it was the first thing I thought of. It's the same color as your hair."

My—what? The fuck—what?

The stranger rose to his feet, pushing back his chair. "I'll see you around, Theodore. Thanks for the great service."

He strolled out of Coffee Boys with his hands in his pockets. The bell over the door tinkled, and a gust of cold autumn air swept into the café after him. I watched him through the window. The sunlight flung a net of gold on his dark glossy hair. When he got to the end of the block, he paused and turned back. I couldn't tell if he was looking at me, but I realized I couldn't move until he had finally vanished around the corner.

I was still clutching his mug of caramel goo in my hand. I shoved it onto the tray with the other dirty dishes and hurried off to the kitchen.

Chapter Two: Extra Sugar

A few days later, I showed up at Coffee Boys to open and was surprised to find a woman already standing outside the doors. She was small and skinny, wearing a cream-colored sweater dress and tall black boots. She had her ash-brown hair pulled back into a messy bun, and her bangs fell into her eyes. She was surrounded by boxes. As I got closer, she waved enthusiastically.

"Theodore! It's been a while! You're as pretty as ever."

"Emma?" I said, laughing in surprise as Klyde's wife lunged at me, wrapping me in a hug that made my bones crack. I flinched. "Jesus, careful. And don't call me *pretty*. I'm not a prize poodle."

"Is Klyde here yet?" Emma said, grinning as she released me. "I told him I'd help put these up today." She gestured at the boxes on the sidewalk.

"What are they?" I asked, unlocking the front doors.

"Halloween decorations, of course. We have to make this place festive for the holidays."

"We sell food here, Emma."

"So?"

"So zombies and spiderwebs aren't exactly appetizing," I said. The mention of Halloween immediately soured my mood.

"I'm not putting up *those* kinds of decorations, Theodore, honestly," she said, rolling her eyes as she stooped and plucked the nearest box from the curb. "I have a bunch of cute ghost decals for the front windows, and I thought we could put some little pumpkins on the tables and..."

She continued to chat excitedly as we brought in all the boxes. I was only half listening, my stomach churning with sudden nausea. I went into the back and started to prepare for the day while Emma bounced around the café, humming to herself as she emptied every single box of its contents.

"Aren't those a fire hazard?" I grumbled, staring up at the orange and yellow lights hanging behind the counter. She had sprinkled plastic pumpkins across the tables too, and fake leaf garlands were bunched around the display cases. "Jesus, Emma. We won't be able to work with all this shit in the way."

"Don't be a party pooper—well look who decided to finally show up." She put her hands on her hips and scowled as Klyde came blustering into the cafe, looking windswept and out of breath.

"God, I'm sorry, babe," he panted. "The twins wouldn't stop bawling when I dropped them off at daycare. I had to stay a bit until they calmed down. That old crone might really throw them out this time."

"No, she won't. We pay her an obscene amount of money." She stepped forward and dropped a light kiss on his cheek, then gestured around the shop. "So? What do you think?"

"You're an artist, my dear."

"Theodore doesn't like it."

"Theodore has a stick up his ass," Klyde said as he shrugged off his coat and hung it up on the coat rack near the espresso machine.

"You're whipped, old man," I said.

"Play nice, boys," Emma said cheerfully. "Honey, will you handle these empty boxes, or do you want me to take them back to the house?"

"I got it. Thanks again, babe. You're the best."

"I know." She stood on tiptoe to receive his kiss. I gagged theatrically behind Klyde's back. She laughed, interrupting their smooch, and Klyde shot me a filthy look. "I'll see you later," she said. "I have some errands to run. It was really nice seeing you again, Theodore."

"Yeah, you too."

The door jingled cheerfully behind her. Klyde sighed dramatically as he stared after her.

"I guess I don't get any morning pick-me-up in the back today."

"Is that a common occurrence?" I demanded, going pale with horror.

"My wife is a giving person, Theodore."

"How did one of the sweetest women on the planet end up with your crusty ass?"

"I know, right? Wait. Have you fallen for her? I'll kill you."

"Don't worry. She's safe from me on account of you know, not having a dick."

Klyde grinned at me as he began placing clean cups onto the countertop.

"So how's *your* love life going?"

"Same as usual."

"Dismal and unpromising?"

"Correct, sir."

Klyde snickered as the doorbell tinkled and a few sleepy-looking professionals wandered inside.

"Time to put on that pretty smile," he said, handing me a yellow apron.

I held it up to my eyes, then looked at him in disbelief. "Why'd you change the color?"

"This is more eye-catching."

"Do I have to wear it?"

"Yeah, dumbass, otherwise you just look like some random freak going around asking people what they want to drink."

I reluctantly tied the apron around my waist, my mood worsening. What had been wrong with the brown ones? They were a lot more practical. First Halloween, then this apron bullshit, and now I had to go and talk to strangers before I was even fully awake. The first thing one of them asked was if they could get a tall iced coffee with no ice.

What a fucking treat this day is going to be.

I was on the floor all morning. I almost tripped over a few of Emma's Halloween decorations, and I barely restrained myself from bursting into an explosive rage and throwing them through the front windows. My feet were killing me and my lower back was on fire. At about 11 o'clock, I was just about to step out for a break—and maybe throw myself into oncoming traffic while I was at it—when the door swung open and I caught a familiar scent sweeping in with the breeze. The professor guy was back. He looked around for a moment until he spotted me. He waved and went to his usual table in the corner.

"He's becoming a regular, isn't he?" Klyde said. He turned towards me and wiggled his eyebrows. "You think he's really here for coffee, or something a little...sweeter? Maybe a pretty green-eyed barista with a foul mouth and a bad attitude?"

"Klyde, if you ever call me pretty again, I'll feed your nut sack to that rabid racoon that hangs out by the dumpster."

"Christ, you're sour." He grinned, then jerked his thumb in the professor's direction. "Want me to take care of him this time?"

"No, it's fine. And you've got the wrong idea anyway. I don't even know his name." I straightened my hideously disappointing apron and marched over to the stranger's table.

Even if he is interested, it's not like it matters.

"Good morning, Theodore." The professor looked up at me as I approached, the sunlight glinting on his glasses.

I could feel Klyde's eyes burning a hole in the back of my head.

"Small coffee with two creams? Or are you going to blow my mind and shake it up today?" My voice sounded more irritated than I'd intended, but he didn't seem to mind.

"Feel free to put in a little sugar. Don't go too crazy, though. I have terrible teeth."

"And a slice of cheesecake?"

"Not this time. I can't afford to embarrass myself in front of you again."

What the hell is supposed to mean? Who cares what anybody in this dive thinks about you?

"Coming right up."

"He ordered some sugar today?" Klyde asked when I was mixing the guy's coffee at the counter. His tone was unbearably smug. "Maybe in more ways than one?"

"Fuck off."

"You can't talk to me like that. You're not my wife."

I ignored him and marched back over to the table. When he reached up to take the mug from me, his cold fingertips grazed my wrist. A bolt of heat shot up my arm when he touched me. I quickly withdrew my hand and fumbled with my apron pockets, making a show of tucking away my pen and notepad.

"How long have you been working here, Theodore?"

"About six months."

"Are you studying at the university?" He smiled when I raised my eyebrows. "You look like a student, that's all."

"I graduated a while ago."

No need to get into the specifics of exactly how many years it had been. My disappointing career path was nobody's business but my own.

"What was your major?"

"Botany."

His eyes went round. "Really?"

"It's not that surprising," I snapped. Then I flushed, hating the petulance I heard in my own voice. "I mean, I know I work here for now, but I had a solid GPA in school and—"

"Oh, I didn't mean to imply you aren't smart," he said quickly. "It's just because of your nails."

I stared at him.

The actual diddly-fuck?

"What do you mean?" I asked, doing my best to sound politely curious instead of annoyed and confused.

"They're always really clean and manicured. You'd think someone who liked working with plants wouldn't have such nice nails." He laughed, looking a little embarrassed as he scratched the back of his neck. "But I guess being a botanist doesn't necessarily mean you have your hands in the dirt all the time, right?"

"Yeah, I don't get into much dirt in a coffee shop," I said, feeling like this conversation was getting away from me. "I'm surprised you noticed."

"Well, you do serve me every day," he said, smiling.

Why is he looking so closely at my hands? Is this like a fetish thing? Is he stalking me? Wait, no, Jesus Christ, Brooks, get it together, you're not worth stalking.

"I guess I'm just kind of obsessive about stuff like that," I heard myself saying.

Why do I feel so hot? Did Klyde turn up the damn heat already? And why are you still standing here, dipshit? There's customers at the counter. Move your ass.

But I continued to remain where I was, staring down at the professor and noticing for the first time that he had the prettiest eyes I'd ever seen. They were the exact same shade of blue as that necklace in *The Titanic* (a movie my mother had watched with the same slavish devotion most people show to an actual god). His thick eyelashes were soot-black and very long. I wondered what he looked like without his glasses.

"Obsessive?" he repeated.

His hair was really nice too. It wasn't as black as I'd thought at first. It was more like maple syrup; the sunshine falling through the window highlighted intermingling threads of amber and gold.

"Dirt in crevices bothers me," I said, laughing a little, and then I almost died from my own cringe.

God, what did that even mean? Too much information, Theodore, you stupid fuck.

I was still running my mouth though, and it didn't help that the professor had leaned forward in his seat and was looking like my bullshit was some of the most interesting stuff he'd heard all day.

"And, um, I have to comb my hair a certain way, and clean my shoes at least once a day when I get home, get any dirt out of the soles and stuff, you know, and then I wash them in the sink..."

Why. Am. I. Still. Talking.

"I never would've guessed you were that finicky about your appearance," he said. "I just thought you were effortlessly pretty."

"What?"

"Theodore," Klyde called out. "The register."

"Yeah, coming!" I shouted, like we weren't two feet away from each other. I turned away from the professor and almost ran back to the counter.

Seriously, could we turn down the fucking heat?

I avoided going back to his table. I pretended to be busy in the back for a while, and when I peeked out to see if he was still around, I saw that Klyde had stepped up and was cleaning away the professor's dirty dishes. I waited a few more minutes before I walked out onto the floor again.

"Done hiding?" Klyde asked, looking up from the register.

"Is he gone?"

"Yeah. You okay? Did he say something weird to you?"

"Nah. I just got caught up with some stuff I had to do in the back," I lied. "I'm gonna step out for some air."

"Okay. You get five minutes. I'll be timing you."

"Fucking tyrant."

"Clock's ticking, peaches."

I thrust my middle finger at him as I slipped out the back door and into the alley behind the shop. I leaned against the brick wall, taking deep breaths. The crisp autumn air was soothing on my hot face. I wiped the sweat from my forehead with the back of a trembling hand.

What the hell was that all about? Is he into me? There's no way, we don't even know each other, and if even if he was, I'm not going out with someone just because he's good looking. I can't put myself through that bullshit again, I'm sick of dating. JESUS, why am I so hot?! It's like thirty fucking degrees out here.

"Theodore?"

Oh fuckballs.

"Oh—uh, hey." I quickly tried to arrange my expression into something normal as I looked up. Sure enough, there was the professor, his hands in the pockets of his long grey coat. "I thought you left."

"I did, but then I saw you out here."

"Oh."

We stared at each other. I suddenly realized how isolated this alleyway was. I had nowhere to run. What if he tried something? What if *I* tried something?

Wait, who the fuck wants to try anything? Christ, has it been that long since you've talked to a good looking guy? Act like a person, dammit!

"I wanted to apologize," the professor said, taking a few steps closer. "I think I came on pretty strong."

I blinked, then pushed myself harder against the wall I was already leaning on, as if I could somehow sink through the bricks and escape the rush of dizzying sensations invoked by his sudden closeness.

Holy shit, wait, so he was for real? He was legit trying to pick me up?

"N-no, it's okay. I was just startled."

He looked at me for a minute longer, his head tilted to the side. Then he held something out to me.

"Will you take this? It's my business card. Sorry, that's all I had on me" He smiled. "But I wrote my number on the back. If you're interested, feel free to call me any time. And I'll stop coming by the café to bother you."

I took the card from him, careful not to brush his fingers again. My brain was a hive of flustered confusion.

"Okay. I feel like I should be honest, though." I took a deep breath before I looked him in the eyes—not an easy task. They turned my stomach into a hot puddle. "I don't think I'll use this. It's nothing personal, it's just—I'm not really into dating right now."

"Oh?" His gaze wandered over my face, tracing the lines of my jaw and mouth before slowly dragging up to meet my eyes again. I felt heat spark in my cheeks and spread down my neck. "Well, keep it anyway," he said softly. "Just in case."

He smiled one more time before he swaggered off down the street. I stared after him with a stupid look on my face, my heart pounding in my ears. After a few minutes, I finally looked down at the card clutched in my limp, sweaty fingers:

Dominic Evans

Licensed Massage Therapist

206-424-7234

4300 9th Avenue, Seattle, WA 98121

Suite 30, 6th Floor

Huh. I was way off about his profession. I flipped the card over, and sure enough, there was a number scribbled there. I stared at it until the digits blurred together. A gust of wind blew my apron up and suddenly I realized that I had probably been out here for way more than five minutes. I hurried back inside, stuffing the card into my pocket.

Chapter Three: Ristretto

Since I didn't work on Halloween, I decided to spend the evening holed up in my apartment doing something decidedly unseasonal: watching *Die Hard* and baking snickerdoodles. Take that, spooky season. I slumped on the couch, munching handfuls of blackened pastries that were more like coasters than cookies. Occasionally I could hear the laughter of trick-or-treaters outside. It did nothing to improve my mood.

Yeah, enjoy it while you can, you little chuckle fucks. It's all downhill from here.

Once the movie ended, I did some mindless chores to take my mind off the merriment going on outside. Then I watered my plants, which honestly felt more like a meditation than a chore. The little green corner in my living room was the only thing in the apartment that brought me any semblance of peace. And because my life was always just a *little* said, I'd named all of them: Don Juan (the pothos curling luxuriously over the windowsill), Scarlett O'Hara (a hardy String of Pearls that had endured more than a few years of transient living), and last but certainly not least, Rasputin (a snake plant that refused to die).

After I was done giving them way too much attention, I sat back down on the couch and finished off two dozen more cookies. Eventually my eyes wandered to Dominic's business card, which was lying on the coffee table. It'd been several days since he gave it to me, and I kept making a note to throw it away. I was currently on a dating hiatus—though maybe "hiatus" wasn't the right word. Technically, you have to still be interested in returning to the original activity in order for it to be called a "hiatus," right? And I had never been less interested in returning to romance. I hadn't gone on a date in years.

And yet, I still had the business card.

My moody reverie was interrupted by a knock on the door. I froze, half a cookie dangling out of my mouth. I heard giggling and scuffling, and then a high voice lisped:

"Trick or Treat!"

Dammit. Some tenants in the building must've let their kids out to make themselves everyone else's problem. Fantastic. I didn't move. After a few more knocks, I heard them shuffle down the hall and knock on some neighboring doors. I sighed. I was going to need something a lot stronger than cookies if I was going to get through the rest of this hellish holiday. I took a carton of beer out of the fridge, popped open the first bottle, and threw it back like a Las Vegas stripper. I managed to drink at least six before I finally passed out on the couch, my head thick with alcohol and my body buzzing with a pleasant numbness. It wasn't my finest hour, but it was still a better Halloween than last year.

As I slept, I dreamed about Daniel again. I woke up in the middle of the night with a raging headache and a face wet with tears.

My parents didn't really accept my sexual orientation—and they both had their own way of showing it.

My mother went out of her way to act like she was okay with it even when it was pretty obvious to everyone around that it made her uncomfortable. Whenever any of her friends asked if I was seeing someone, she would interject with a loud laugh and say in frantically cheerful voice: "Keep your girls away, ladies, this one likes boys!" This kind of desperation showed up in smaller things too. If a pretty actress appeared on T.V., she would start gushing about her good looks, only to stop short and look over at me with an apologetic smile. "Oh, I'm sorry, dear, you aren't interested in that sort of thing, are you?" She never asked what kind of men I liked, or whether or not I was dating anyone. In fact, she stopped asking me about my love life at all.

As for my father, well, he was…old school. He started his own landscaping business when he was eighteen because he believed every man should be self-made; he thought therapy was a scam and that most people "just needed to exercise more"; he thought veganism was the next great American health crisis; and he was suspicious of "metrosexuals" (defined by him as any man who wore hair gel or pastels). When I told him I was gay, he looked at me for the longest minute of my life and then said gruffly: "Alright, kiddo." And that was that. His silence settled on my shoulders like concrete weights. It was as bad as open disapproval, and it made me feel just as shitty. For years, the unspoken "problem" of my sexuality lurked like mold beneath every interaction I had with my parents. Everything finally boiled over one year ago on Halloween. That also the last time I saw Daniel.

Daniel was a friend I met in college. He was a red-faced, beefy blonde with a nose shaped like a ham. We met in sophomore year and hit it off right away because we both bitched about the same things. We formed a study group and it was a lot of fun—though to be honest, it involved more drinking than studying. Daniel could really put away his booze. It took exactly thirteen shots and three beers until he started to get off balance and hit on everything that moved—including trees and parked cars. Usually I escaped such advances, though one time he tried to kiss me because he thought I was someone named "Thelma."

"God, I'm sorry," he groaned the next morning when he was nursing a giant hangover. "You looked just like a girl. You're way too pretty for a dude."

"If you were in less pain, I'd slap the shit out of you right now," I said as I passed him a bottle of water and a handful of migraine pills.

We stayed friends after graduating, meeting about once a month to catch up. Last year, we decided to go to a Halloween party together. I was staying with my folks over the holiday weekend, so Daniel picked me up and we drove there together. By the end of the night, Daniel was, unsurprisingly, kind of drunk. I drove us back to my parents and told him to come inside and sober up for a bit before he went home. We staggered into the dark house, and as I fumbled for a light, Daniel fell down on the couch, snickering at nothing in particular.

"Hey Thelma," he crooned, "walk that nice ass over here."

"Shut up, asshole. You'll wake up my parents. I'll go get you some water."

"Aw c'mon, I know it's you, Theoooo...."

"You are *shit* faced, dude."

"Thanks for drivin', Thelma, you're such a peach. Hey, lookie what I got." From the depths of his cavernous coat, Daniel pulled out a can of beer. He cracked it open and took a few gulps before thrusting it towards me, a silly grin on his face. "Want some?"

"No thanks. And I brought you here to sober up. Gimmie that."

"Booooo."

I snatched the beer from his hand. I'd been expecting him to have a tighter grip and so I pulled it away with greater force than necessary. Some beer slopped over the lip over the can and sloshed onto my hands.

"Shit."

"Woopsie! Careful, Thelma."

"Let go. Are you nuts?"

He was snickering and pulling at my sleeve. I lost my balance, cursed, and fell on top of him just as the overhead light switched on. We both shot up, peering in confusion over the back of the couch.

My parents were standing in the doorway, their faces pale and horrified.

It took me a second to register what it was they thought they were seeing. I felt a wad of nausea curdle in my stomach.

"Theodore, who is this?" Dad said in a deadly quiet voice.

"This is my friend Daniel," I said, weakly gesturing at the drunk on the couch. Daniel was squinting at my parents like he wasn't sure they were real.

"'Lo," he said thickly, giving them a boozy smile.

If possible, my mother went paler, and my dad's scowl deepened. I could feel my ears burning, which I'm sure incriminated me further in their eyes. Then Dad turned and left the room without a word. Mom looked at me, her mouth drawn into such a tight line that it was practically nonexistent.

"Honestly," she whispered, shaking her head. Then she left too.

I stood there for a few seconds, then I went after them, leaving Daniel to sleep it off on the couch.

"Wait a second," I said, catching up with them at the foot of the stairs. "It isn't what you think."

"And how do you know what I think, Theodore?" Dad said, his nostrils flaring.

"Dear—" Mom said frantically, but he ignored her and went on.

"You parade a strange man who stinks of booze into my living room in the middle of the goddamned night—"

"He's just a friend, Dad. He drank too much at the party so I was letting him sober up before he went home. That's all."

"You expect me to believe that?"

"What?"

"If you have a boyfriend, the least you could do is have the balls to tell me to my face like a man."

I stared at him, and then I looked over at my mother. Her gaze was fixed to the side, on some indeterminable point in space, and she was fiddling with her collar. She said nothing. Then I understood. If I was straight, my dad would've probably laughed the incident off. After all, he'd had plenty of drunk nights with his own friends when he was younger. But because I was gay, the situation was automatically shrouded in promiscuity.

My embarrassment gave way to anger.

"Being gay doesn't mean I fuck everything that moves," I snapped.

"Don't talk to us like that," Dad snarled, but I'd had enough of his bullshit. I turned without another word and walked back into the living room. Daniel was sitting up and staring at me.

"Get up," I said. "I'll drive you home and then take an Uber back or something."

He didn't argue as he rolled off the couch and followed me out of the front door. Neither of us spoke as we climbed into his car and drove off. The shadows from the trees on either side of the street filled the car like gray phantoms.

"You're gay?" he said after a long silence.

Something in his tone made me grip the steering wheel so hard my knuckles went white.

"Yup," I said tersely.

"I didn't know." We were silent for a minute longer. Then he said: "I tried to kiss you when I was drunk, man."

"It's no big deal. You were out of it."

"Were you like...*into* it, though?"

"What?"

He turned his face towards the window. "Forget it."

I pulled up to his apartment a few minutes later. I put the brake on and then climbed out. Daniel heaved himself out of the passenger side, and we then looked at each other from over the car roof.

"I'm sorry you had to put up with that," I said.

He shrugged. "Hey, every family has their stuff, right?"

"Do you want help getting inside?"

"Nah."

I watched him walk unsteadily up the sidewalk. I thought about running after him and explaining to him that I didn't like him that way. That his weird drunken exploits were no big deal, that he didn't need to feel awkward around me. But I didn't move. Daniel let himself into his building and shut the door. I stood there for a while before I remembered I needed to call a ride. It came in a matter of seconds. As I climbed into the back seat and gave the driver my address (I decided to collect my things from my parents' house another day), I realized my hands felt weird. The beer, I thought suddenly. I'd never washed it off. Now that I noticed it, I couldn't ignore the way it felt on my skin. It was like I was wearing thick, sticky gloves. I picked at the residue with my nails, but I only managed to make myself bleed. I stuck my hands in my pockets, hoping the driver hadn't noticed.

The car rolled down the road in silence until it finally pulled up at my own apartment. I checked the clock on the dash. It had taken exactly twenty-one minutes to get from Daniel's place to mine. Had it always been that far away? I got out with a brief farewell to the driver, walked quickly into the building, and rode the elevator up to my floor. As soon as I unlocked my door, I went straight to the sink and stuck my bloodied hands under the faucet.

I texted Daniel a few times after that night, but he never responded. I hadn't heard from him since.

I blinked in the harsh sunlight streaming through the living room window. I slowly sat up, wincing as my head throbbed in protest. The coffee table was littered with empty beer bottles.

Well done, Brooks. A real winner of a night. Way to wallow in self-pity, asshole.

I swept the bottles into a recycling bag and then spent the next five minutes scrubbing the coffee table where some beer had trickled out. After the table had been cleaned to my liking, and my hands were red and raw from working the sponge too hard, I staggered to my feet and went to the kitchen. I popped open my kitchen cabinets to grab coffee, only to remember that I had run out the other day.

Fuckballs.

My head was starting to throb. After a moment's deliberation, I went to get my house keys. There was a convenience store around the corner. I could get coffee there, and some migraine pills while I was at it.

It was unseasonably warm out, which was great because I was halfway down the block before I realized that I forgot to grab my coat on the way out the door. The same maroon sweatshirt I'd been wearing last night was more than enough; it smelled glamorously of spilled beer and regret.

The bell that tingled over the door when I entered the store rang very loudly in my post-booze brain. I winched, scurrying to the medicine aisle and cursing the brightness of the fluorescent lights.

"No, that one there..."

"Here? But it's the wrong color."

The people in the aisle next to mine had loud voices that carried. I resisted the urge to lob something at them from over the shelves as I bent down to look at the medicine options. I wanted something that could knock out a horse.

"That one's too pricey," said a man's voice.

"I'm gonna pay for it myself, so hand it over." The other voice sounded young and shrill.

"Since when do you pay for anything?"

"Since Dad gave me an increase in my allowance last week."

"Yeah, ten extra cents is just what you need to buy—is this what I think it is, Hannah? Did you seriously drag my ass down here to buy tampons? You said it was an emergency."

"Um, yeah. I think leaving a trail of blood wherever I go constitutes an emergency, asshole. Mom had the car."

"You know I have a job, right?"

I dipped my head to get better look at the meds on the bottom shelf. There was a gap between some of the bottles and I could see into the other aisle. I found myself staring at two pairs of feet: one in familiar-looking black shoes, the other in dark green booties. They continued to bicker about the delights and hurdles of menstruation while I did my best to block them out. I finally found what I needed after a few minutes. When I straightened up, pills in hand, I realized their conversation had turned to dating—a subject I was definitely not interested in hearing about. I started to move away.

"Why not? I think you'd like him!"

"I won't bore you with the plethora of reasons for why being set up by a sixteen-year-old girl is weird. Personally, it's the whole 'you're my sister' thing that's really sticking a cog in the wheel for me."

"It's not *that* weird."

"I'm interested in someone else anyway, so I'll pass. Appreciate the creepy thought, though."

"Wait, wait, *what*? Oh my God, for real? Who? Where? Tell me everything!"

"There's nothing to tell. He hasn't even called me yet....he probably won't."

"Wait, then like...this is nothing. You literally got me excited over nothing, Dominic."

"*You* got yourself excited over nothing."

"Wait, do you just say he's gonna call *you*? *You* gave him *your* number? What's his name? What does he do? Oh my God—"

"You need to take a few breaths. You're foaming at the mouth."

"Sorry. It's just so—"

"Jesus. Go buy your tampons."

I heard both pairs of feet moving down the aisle and I felt my limbs jolt to life. I made a beeline for the door, throwing the migraine pills I'd been planning to buy at the head of the bewildered cashier as I fled out into the street. I ran the rest of the way back to my place. It was only when I had slammed the door to my apartment that exhaustion finally hit and I collapsed into a sweaty heap on the floor.

It took several minutes for my body to calm down and my brain to process what had just happened.

What the literal fuck? How desperate do you have to be to wait around for someone you know isn't gonna call? Why would anyone hold onto hope for that long?

I pulled myself up from the floor and went over to the couch. I flopped down on the well-worn cushions and stared at my feet for several minutes. Eventually my eyes traveled to the card lying on the coffee table. I hesitated, then picked it up and dialed the number on the back before giving myself a chance to second guess the decision.

It rang three times before he picked up.

"Hello?"

My bravado incinerated like twigs in a bonfire. Panicking, I hung up, threw my phone on the couch, and then stared at it like it was a snake that was going to rear up and bite me. I almost jumped out of my pants when it started to ring. I stared at it, wide-eyed. Then I took a deep breath and picked it up again. I opened my mouth to speak, but nothing came out.

"Hello?" Dominic said again. The sound of his voice ransacked my body with an unexpected rush of emotion. "Is this Theodore?"

"Uh, y-yeah, hi."

"Hi there." He sounded like he was smiling.

"Sorry it took so long to call."

"I'm just glad you did. What can I do for you?"

Why does my tongue feel like a fucking life-sized ham in my mouth right now? Words, what are those? Jesus, say SOMETHING, he's waiting!

It was only then that I suddenly remembered I had never asked anyone out before.

"W-would you like to do something?" I wanted to slap myself across the face.

"Yes, very much. When?"

"Um, well, I get off work tomorrow at six. Did you want to come by the cafe? We can go to dinner if you want."

Wait, no, shit, if he comes by the store Klyde will see him and—

"That sounds great."

"Okay, cool."

I wonder what it would be like to get through a sentence sounding competent?

"See you later then, Theodore."

There was an odd intimacy to the way he said those words. A hot shiver passed through me.

"Y-Yeah. Yeah. See you soon, Dominic."

His name tasted like honey on my tongue.

Chapter Four: After Hours

I was oddly disconnected from the usual bullshit at work the next day. I was nervous about meeting Dominic later, but I was also...excited? I hadn't looked forward to going out with someone in years, so honestly, I wasn't sure if I was feeling excited or just nauseous. Maybe it was both.

"Good work today," Klyde said, grinning at me from behind the counter where he was wiping down mugs. "You only had *two* breakdowns in the back."

"Yeah, thanks," I said distractedly, shrugging into my coat as I glanced towards the door.

"That's it?"

"Sorry?"

"What's your problem? I'm baiting you here."

"And I'm ignoring your bullshit."

"Uh-oh. Look who it is."

Klyde nodded towards the window. I followed his gaze and then cursed inwardly. Dominic was fifteen minutes early, leaning against a tree growing by the curb. I wasn't sure if he was deliberately putting himself on display, but it was impossible that he didn't know how good looking he was, right? My God. It was a public safety hazard.

"What's he doing here?" Klyde demanded. "He knows we're closed, right? Is he still bothering you? I'm calling the cops."

"Relax. He's...here for me."

"*What?*"

"I'll see you tomorrow," I said, moving towards the door, my ears burning.

"Um, details? Hey, c'mon!"

I almost flung myself out of the café and onto the main sidewalk. The door jingled behind me. Dominic looked up. Our eyes met, and my stomach jolted like I'd missed a step going downstairs.

"Hi," we said at the same time. Cue awkward pause. Then I gestured to the restaurant across the street; it was a Japanese place that had taken more than one of my paychecks. "How do you feel about sushi?"

"I like it. And I've been wanting to try that place for a while, actually."

"Yeah, they're really good."

"Any recommendations?"

"Um, I guess the California roll is pretty good...though that's not actually sushi, is it?"

"Me and my college friends called anything on rice sushi...but we were also broke and dumb and willing to eat anything short of literal garbage. So you're asking the wrong guy."

I laughed as we came to the curb and waited for the crosswalk signal to change. "Where did you go to school?"

"The Pittsburgh School of Massage Therapy."

"What got you into massage?"

"I guess I thought that if I was going to be spending eight hours doing something, I wanted it to be on making people feel better. It surely had nothing to do with the fact that I was too stupid to get into real."

"Yeah, you missed out. It's a real shame choosing a trade people actually want to buy rather than sinking thousands of dollars into a degree you'll never use."

"You sound a little bitter, Theodore."

"That would be an accurate summation of the events as they currently stand."

He grinned. There was a slight pause in the conversation, then he said: "How long ago was college for you, anyway?"

"What?"

"You look very young."

"I'm twenty-seven," I said, a tad resentfully.

He seemed to notice my bitchy tone. "I didn't mean it in a bad way," he said quickly.

"So how old are you, then?"

"Twenty-three."

I stared at him. "And you already have your own massage practice?"

He shrugged. "I got lucky. I found a cheap building."

Well shit. Here I was, walking around with coffee in one hand and my dick in the other, while Dominic was out there running his own business and not paying off copious amounts of debt.

"I guess between the two of us, the numbers even out, right?" he said, smiling down at me.

The crosswalk signal finally changed, which gave me a good excuse to look away from him for a second. We crossed the street, narrowly avoiding death at the hands of rage-filled Seattle drivers as we stumbled into the restaurant.

It wasn't very crowded and so we got a table right away. It was in the corner, tucked away from the busier part of the restaurant, and a bit snug. Dominic's legs stretched over into my foot territory, and so he angled himself so he could position them to the side.

"That can't be comfortable," I said, raising my eyebrows over the menu I had in my hands.

He grinned. "Believe it or not, I'm used to being too large for the world in general and making the appropriate adjustments."

"I've never had that problem. Guess I'm too dainty."

"I guess you are," he said softly.

If he keeps on looking at me like that I'm going to be in serious danger of throwing my pants at his head. Jesus, get it together, it's the first date, and it's not like you'd even know what to do after that, dumbass, just take a deep fucking breath.

We ordered a few dishes to share. I got my usual California roll and then flirted briefly with death by trying wasabi for the first time. One glass of water wasn't enough to quell the subsequent fire that raged on my tongue and in my nose. Dominic calmly passed me his own glass.

"Easy," he said, looking like he was holding back a laugh while I coughed. "It'd be a shame for you to die on the first date."

"So there will be others?" I asked.

A second later I felt my insides shrivel with embarrassment. I felt my cheeks reddening and I scrambled for something to say to take it back. But before I could, Dominic reached over and placed his long fingers over the back of the hand I had resting on the table.

"That's up to you."

I stared for a full thirty seconds into his face; every bone in my body grew warm and soft.

"I mean, I'm pretty sure you also have a say," I said weakly.

He smiled and removed his hand. His touch left my skin tingling.

"I'd like that very much." He held my gaze for a moment, then he said slowly: "Listen, Theodore, I...I don't mean to be a tease or anything. It's just that in the past I've come on pretty strong. I don't want to do that with you."

"Oh." I looked down at my plate. "So...you're okay with taking it slow?"

"Of course. I'll let you set the pace."

Will he really be satisfied with letting me crawl along? I'm already regretting this, I never should've called, he probably has other irons in the fire anyway, this is such a waste of time for him—

"Are you okay?" he asked, frowning.

"I guess I'm wondering what you're looking for here."

"What do you mean?"

"I'm not really a dating around kind of guy," I mumbled.

This was so embarrassing to talk about. How could I say *I don't want to share you* to a guy I just met? It sounded so childish.

"Are you asking me if there's anyone else?" When I didn't answer, his voice softened. "Look at me, Theodore."

"Why?"

It's much easier to just stare at this table and stew in my own awkwardness.

"Well, for starters, I want to see your beautiful eyes."

What a cheap shot, hitting me with that when I already can't think straight.

But I found myself obeying. "Yours aren't bad either," I said, coloring hotly beneath their intense stare.

He smiled. "Look, I'm not much of a date-around guy either. I'd like to have you all to myself—if that's alright with you."

I felt my face grow even hotter.

"Okay," I said. My voice came out hoarse and shaky. I cleared my throat.

"Okay?" he repeated.

"Yeah, let's do it."

"Should we shake on it or something?"

"I think a verbal agreement can suffice."

He grinned as he reached into his pocket. "Let me pay for half of dinner."

My head snapped up, all traces of bashfulness suddenly gone. "No way."

"But I—"

"I may be working a minimum wage job and heading nowhere in life, but I said I'd take you out. If you so much as reach for that check, we're over."

He raised both hands into the hair like he was surrendering to a pit pocket.

"Flawless logic."

"You bet your ass it is."

He grinned again just as the waitress came over with our check. Like a good boy, he didn't reach for it. After we had paid and walked out of the restaurant, we paused for a moment on the sidewalk. I had the rather startling revelation that I didn't want to say goodnight just yet.

"Do you want to take a walk around the block?" I said hesitantly.

"Sure. It's a nice night."

We set off, strolling side by side on a relatively empty stretch of city block. It was a cold and starless night, but a full moon was out, hanging above our heads like a great shining coin. I stole side glances at him as we walked. Beneath the glow of the streetlamps, his dark hair looked lighter, almost chestnut. I really liked his shoulders too. They looked so solid and warm. I wondered what it would be like to rest my head on them.

"Do I have something in my teeth?" Dominic asked.

I averted my gaze.

"Just spacing out. So how long have you lived in Seattle?"

"I'm from here originally. I came back after I graduated in Pittsburgh. I never liked the idea of being too far away from my family."

"You guys are close then?"

"Sometimes painfully so," he said, laughing.

"Do you have siblings?"

"I'm the oldest of six."

"Jesus," I said, staring off into the darkness and trying to think of something else to say. But the only thing that came out was another robust, "*Jesus.*"

"Yup. Two younger sisters and three younger brothers."

"God bless."

"What about you?"

"I'm an only child."

"Lucky son of a bitch."

I grinned. "That comes with its downsides too. I'm the only kid my parents have to deal with. That can be a bit...overwhelming."

"I get that. Are you originally from this area too?"

"Yeah, I went to college in Oregon but moved back here after to live out my dream of serving coffee to strangers."

He laughed as we circled the corner and headed back towards Coffee Boys. "You said you studied botany, right? What did you wanna do with it? Like lab research?"

His words scraped at the edges of old wounds. I felt the old disappointment rising inside of me, the tired, familiar sense of failure and inadequacy.

"I wanted to get into field work," I said quietly. "But every place I applied to wanted at least five years of experience, and I couldn't get that experience because no one would give me a job, and so I just ran around in circles until I lost steam. I did some copywriting for a bit, but writing about botany just depressed me even more because it reminded me that I wasn't out there actually *doing* it."

"That sounds frustrating."

I shrugged. I didn't need or want his pity. "Yeah, well. It's my fault for picking such a niche field."

"What got you interested in botany in the first place?"

I paused for a second before responding. "My dad owns a landscaping business. He used to take me along on jobs when I was a kid."

"Did you want to take over the family business?"

"Not really." He didn't ask me to elaborate—which made me feel more comfortable with doing so. "I guess...I liked the stubborn beauty of plants. They can thrive in the worst environments. Like there's a plant called purple saxifrage that grows in both Arctic *and* mountainous areas. You'd never know by looking at it that it's so hearty. It looks really delicate. And of course there's succulents, which are my favorite. They grow where life shouldn't even exist. And there's this other plant called Welwitschia that's native to the Namib desert and Southern Angola. It's one of the ugliest things you'll ever see in your life, but it'll outlive all of us. It's estimated that some of them are over a thousand years old. I mean that's insane. I—-"

I stopped, feeling embarrassment creep over me. I had rambled for so long that our walk was over, and we had arrived at our initial starting point.

God, did I really go on for that long about weeds? Welp, this is it, our first and last date.

"Sorry," I said quickly, back peddling so fast I was in danger of falling off my own existential cliff. "None of this is interesting."

"It is." He smiled down at me, a sudden tenderness in his eyes. "You're very passionate about it."

He looked so impressed that I felt myself reddening.

"Do you need a ride home?" I mumbled.

"Nah, I brought my car. But thank you for tonight, Theodore. I had a really nice time."

"Can I...call you later?" The words were out of my mouth before I could really think about them.

"You can call me anytime."

We stood there looking at each other for a moment. Dominic made a small movement, as if he meant to step towards me, but then he turned away, raising his hand in farewell.

"Good night, Theodore."

"'Night."

My eyes followed him as he crossed the street. It was twenty degrees out, but I felt very warm. The flush on my face had spread to the rest of my body. My skin vibrated with a nervous heat as I watched Dominic get into his car and pull away.

I did call him again, and we went out the next day. And the day after that. Before I knew it, the trees outside the front window at Coffee Boys had shed their coppery hoods. The naked branches twisted towards a pearly sky, which was perpetually on the verge of expelling the season's first snow. The temperatures dropped, and as a result, Coffee Boys experienced a nice surge on hot drink sales.

My days flowed so smoothly I was in danger of being content. It was easy being with Dominic—too easy. I expected something to go wrong at any second, the revealing of some seedy detail that couldn't be forgiven. But no matter how hard I looked, there was nothing to alarm me. There was only stuff to like. I guess if I was forced to pick a flaw, I might say he was too smooth of a talker—which doesn't sound too bad until you're on the other end of it.

For example, Exhibit A:

Lately we had been partaking in "brunch bouncing"—his term, not mine. This sounded like the gay equivalent of bar hopping to me, but I soon discovered that it was actually something he'd done with his massage friends back in school. He took me to some pretty fancy places. Whenever I tried to split the check, he always waved my money away.

"I have to repay you for the sushi, right?" he said.

"What're you talking about?" I demanded. "I'm sure you've already gone way over what I spent."

"If it bothers you that much, I'll let you pay for the next one."

"That's what you said last time."

"Did I?" he asked innocently.

"I think you just like feeling superior, Mr. Evans."

"I think I just like *you*, Mr. Brooks."

What the hell was I supposed to say to that? I had nothing, although I do think I turned the color of a fire truck. You know. Like an adult.

He was always saying stuff like that, casually lobbing compliments like bombs into our conversations. True to our agreement, he hadn't made a single move on me, but these verbal sneak attacks left me just as flustered as physical contact probably would have. I was continually amazed at his utter lack of self-consciousness. He seemed to have no problem saying whatever he felt. I couldn't decide if this made him admirable or psycho.

Whatever it was...I didn't hate it.

It felt like Halloween had barely ended, but it was already almost Thanksgiving. Dominic was going home, and I wasn't sure what I was doing. I'd received a text from Mom a few days earlier, asking me what my plans were for the holiday. I hadn't been back to the house since the whole Halloween fiasco, and she'd made repeated attempts to mend bridges, calling me every month and attempting to have at least some semblance of a relationship. Sometimes she would put her phone on speaker so my dad could join in the conversation. My interactions with him were always awkward and stilted, and he never initiated a call himself. Neither did I.

Dominic happened to be present for the most recent of these uncomfortable calls. When I hung up, he looked at me with raised eyebrows (glancing up from the bowl of popcorn he'd been consuming in front of my T.V.) and asked if everything was alright.

"Why wouldn't it be?"

"Hmm. That's not what I asked." The side of his mouth pulled up into a wry smile.

"Well appreciate my tactful avoidance of your question, then." My irritable tone only made his smile widen. I sighed. "Things are just weird with my parents right now."

"You can come home with me if you like."

Oh, God, that's just what I need, to be the random at a family dinner full of total strangers. Also that's kind of fast, isn't it? We haven't been going out that long...

"No, that's okay, I'll figure something out."

I waited for him to ask for more details, but he just patted the seat next to him and redirected his gaze to the T.V.

"Let me know if you change your mind. I'd be happy to show you off."

I rolled my eyes as I flopped next to him. It took me a second to realize what he was watching.

"Is this *Lost*?"

"They've been playing reruns for the last few nights."

"Did you lose a bet or something?"

He snickered. "I never watched it the first time it came out."

"Well buckle up for a mediocre ride."

"Has anyone ever told you that you're a tad negative?"

"What an astute study of character you are. You should—-"

He grinned and shoved a handful of popcorn into my mouth.

"Shut that beautiful mouth."

"Oohf daf moorst!" My clever retort was lost in the wads of popcorn crammed into my cheeks. I felt my eyes watering as I struggled to swallow.

"Hey, by the way, are you busy tomorrow? There's a new vegetarian brunch place downtown. I'd like to take you."

"I can't believe you're asking me out after openly abusing me like this," I said, wiping my mouth with the back of my hand as I glared at him.

"I don't hear you saying no."

He reached over and slipped another piece of popcorn between my lips—gently this time. His fingertips brush against my tongue, and I tasted the sweetness of his skin.

"I'll pick you up at eleven," he said.

"Okay," I said in a voice that came out a lot tinier and squeakier than I'd intended.

I learned the next morning that the brunch place was actually a restaurant Klyde had mentioned a few days ago. It was called "The Veggie Patch," and as we approached, I noticed even from across the street that it was already jam packed with beanie-wearing hipsters. Not a great start. I hoped they at least had a decent eggs benedict.

The crosswalk signal changed; as we attempted to cross the street, a group of bicycling teenagers burst around the corner. We stumbled out of their way just in time. They hooted and laughed over their shoulders as they pedaled down the road. I willed them to crash and die, but they rode off into the distance without so much as a smoking tire.

Assholes. I hate kids—no, I hate anyone who rides a two-wheeled vehicle around in public. Bikes, motorcycles, whatever, it gives them all such a sense of entitlement—

"Are you okay?" Dominic asked. His voice called me back to our present situation—and the position we were in.

In our haste to clear the bikers, we had fallen against the brick facade of one of the many little shops that lined the streets downtown. I was leaning against his chest, and both his hands were resting lightly on my waist. I could feel the warmth of his skin radiating through his thin black sweater. He smelled absolutely unreal. My God, was it cologne? Or was it just his natural scent? It saturated my lungs and lingered on my tongue. I started to feel hot and dizzy.

"Theodore," he said in a strained voice. "I meant what I said before about going at your pace." His breath tickled my eyelashes as he leaned over me. "But touching you makes me forget my own name, so let's keep a respectable distance, hm?" He gently pushed me away, ruffled my hair, and then strode past me. "Let's hurry up so we can get a good seat. You're still hungry, right?"

Sure, because nothing quells blue balls like brunch.

I followed him slowly, wondering how on earth I was supposed to focus on food after *that*. Turns out I managed alright. The eggs benedict proved to be a worthy distraction.

The day after Dominic went home for the holiday, I got a package in the mail. My first totally rational thought was that it was a bomb. My second totally rational thought was that I wasn't worth bombing. I opened it suspiciously.

Inside was a small cut of what I instantly recognized as *crassula ovata*—a jade plant. Enclosed was a small card with Dominic's scrawl. I opened it, my heart hammering.

Stubbornly beautiful, like someone else I know. I'll see you after Thanksgiving.

—Dominic

Chapter Five: No Whipped Cream

"Excuse me, young man," an old woman called out as I crossed the floor.

I'd been on my way to the counter to put in a few orders, but I made a detour to her table, bracing myself. It was way too early in the morning to deal with the bullshit I was sure was coming my way. Thanksgiving was over (I'd spent it eating potato chips on the couch and watching football), and the pumpkins and leaves in the coffee shop had been swapped for evergreen garlands and artificial Christmas trees. Emma seemed to have an endless supply of seasonal decor. It was irritating.

"Yes ma'am?"

"I ordered this caramel latte and asked for no whipped cream. Well, as you can see, this has quite a bit on it."

"Sorry about that. I'll get you another one right now."

I collected her mug and marched back to the counter. Once I got there, I checked the details of her order: Tall caramel latte with whipped cream and soy milk. No note to omit any ingredients. Yup. That sounded about right.

"Hey, that's a crime against nature," Klyde protested when he saw me dumping the coffee into the sink.

"She wants one with no whipped cream."

"What the hell? That's like a sexless marriage."

"Not everyone would find a sexless marriage to be a bad thing, Klyde."

"To each their own, I suppose," he said with a heavy sigh.

I felt the back of my neck reddening and I hoped he wouldn't notice. Luckily some customers approached the register, and he was sufficiently distracted.

It was pretty quiet the rest of the day, which was good news for me. I didn't really have my head in the game. I was thinking a lot about Dominic—or rather, I was thinking about the feelings that had taken root inside of me ever since he sent me that jade plant. They were confusing—and they scared me.

I wasn't a *total* noob when it came to romance, but I could count on one hand the experience I did have, and I could do it on less than five fingers. The first time I'd been intimate with someone was five years ago. It was a fast and feverish incident that left me feeling like discarded goods. I had just gone along with the guy because I was grateful anyone would want to do anything with me in the first place. He didn't talk to me afterwards. That jaded me for a bit and I

went into hiding for a few years. When I did tentatively poke my head out of the closet again, the person I decided to take a chance on ended up being a guy who was looking for a distraction from his rocky marriage—all of this reported to me after more than a few intimacies. They had never crossed the final line into sex, but they'd still meant quite a lot to me.

After that fiasco, I decided I was better off alone. Anything was better than constant humiliation and disappointment.

Then Dominic had waltzed into my personal space, and I couldn't shake the idea that maybe it would be different with him. Which was stupid. Because it wouldn't. It never was. I reminded myself that the last time I had let my guard down, I found myself sitting at the bottom of the stairs, crying my eyes out because some douchebag got what he wanted from me and then hung me out to dry.

Don't get carried just because he gave you a plant. It's not worth it.

We stayed open a little later than usual in the hopes of coaxing in new customers. But after the clock ticked to seven, Klyde finally gave up and locked the doors.

"I wonder if Emma will still love me if we're homeless."

"Jesus, Klyde, it was one slow day," I said, wandering around the cafe and collecting the empty dishes on the tables. I piled them all on a tray and then went back to the counter, plopping it down in front of him.

Klyde sighed and began to load the little plates and mugs into the dishwasher. "She's accustomed to a certain lifestyle."

"So pay me more and I can help her keep it."

"You think I'm made of money or something?"

"Cheap ass."

"If you keep talking sweet like that, my marriage might be in real trouble." He grinned and tossed me a rag. "Wipe the tables down for me."

I rolled my eyes as I caught it and got to work. We spent a few moments in silence before Klyde said:

"So how's it going?"

I looked up from the booth I was wiping down. "Er...fine?"

"I mean with that guy. What was it? Damien?"

I immediately resumed wiping, angling myself so that he couldn't see my face. "Dominic. And it's fine."

"Just fine?"

"Yup. Things are peaches and cream."

"See, that makes me think that things are not, in fact, peaches and cream."

I moved on to the next booth. I heard the clinking of dishes as Klyde resumed cleaning. After a few minutes I turned around to face him.

"You don't have to worry about me."

"I know. You just seemed distracted today. I wanted to make sure you were okay."

I paused. I felt my skin growing warm. "I'm just...worried."

"About what?"

"About stuff I've been...feeling."

"Like?" His tone was maddeningly patient. I wondered if this was his "dad" voice.

"Well...my other relationships have had...um..."

"*What*?"

"No whipped cream," I blurted out. Then I wanted to bang my head on the table until I lost consciousness.

"What the hell're you—-" I watched his expression change as he gradually understood what I was saying. Then he shook his head and sighed. "Are you in middle school? Jesus, man. Just say you've never had sex."

"It's not an easy thing to bring up," I snapped, my face blazing.

Klyde leaned against the counter, crossing his arms over his chest and clearly waiting for me to elaborate. I searched for the words, but I couldn't find them. I already regretted bringing it up.

"Me and Emma had a pretty weird relationship before we got married," Klyde said after the silence had continued for several seconds. "We were together for three years and we even lived together for a bit. But we didn't have sex until after the ceremony. There were plenty of people who thought that was a mistake. I had a buddy of mine say he would never be comfortable committing without taking a test drive first—talking about Emma like she was a fuckin' bus or something." He shook his head again. "But we wanted to build up to it. That was our choice. My point is that a relationship can look however you want it to look, Theodore. That includes sex. Nobody is entitled to your junk just because you've gone out to dinner a handful of times."

"I know that."

"Is he pressuring you?"

"He hasn't even brought it up."

"So is sex something *you're* interested in?"

"I don't know. I've never wanted to have it before."

"And now you do?"

"I'm not sure. I still don't know him very well."

"So take your time figuring things out. What's the rush? You're still a snot-nosed brat. You've got all the time in the world." He grinned, and then jabbed his finger at me. "Now finish cleaning up and get the hell out of here. I can't afford to pay you overtime."

The Christmas season in downtown Seattle was always a breathtaking sight. Every tree which lined the block was decked up in lights. Several businesses installed spotlights on the facade of their buildings so that when it was dark, the structures appeared as if they were glowing from the inside out, creating a mirage of emerald, crimson, and gold. The park usually had a giant Christmas tree erected, and the feathery green boughs reached up towards the sky in a glittering tower of baubles and lights.

Coffee Boys joined the festivities, albeit mildly. Emma strung some twinkling snowflake lights around the front window, and two Nutcracker Santas the size of small children flanked the front door. There was also an incessant loop of Christmas music playing inside the cafe, and Emma's insistence that all the staff wear Santa hats. I strongly protested to Klyde, but in a twist that shocked no one, he disregarded my opinion and sided with his wife.

"Emma thinks you look especially cute in one," he said.

"Like a little Christmas elf," Emma chimed in, beaming as she popped up from behind his shoulder, carrying a tray of mugs. "Would you be willing to wear bells on your shoes too, Theodore?"

"That depends, Emma. Would you be willing to be mentioned in my subsequent suicide note?"

"Jesus. What did your parents do to you?"

"Probably more than they'll ever know."

"You're not going home for the holidays, then?" Klyde asked, grinning.

"No idea." I spotted some new customers entering the shop, and I began to move away from the counter.

"Ooooh, or are you spending it with the boy toy?" Klyde said.

"Boy toy?" Emma repeated. "Is that the glasses guy you mentioned before, honey?"

"Bingo, baby. Seems that him and our little Christmas elf are quite besotted with one another."

"Wow. Is this what they call a Christmas miracle?"

"It sure it is, sweet cheeks—hey, don't run off," Klyde called after me while his wife collapsed against him in a fit of cackling.

I walked away from them as fast I could without actually running. I wished I could hibernate for the rest of the month and escape the pressure of spending the holidays with loved ones. I was still deciding what Dominic was, and as for my parents—well, that didn't seem promising. Mom had called me on Thanksgiving, and through my vague answers, she figured out that I wasn't celebrating the turkey day with friends after all. I was just not celebrating.

"So let me see if I understand this," she said, her voice reaching a pitch that I recognized as the escalation before the storm. "You would rather do nothing for the holiday than come home?"

"Honestly, Mom? Yeah."

"Honey, what do you want from us? I call you all the time, don't I? And your father loves you. It's just...complicated. Please be patient."

"Great. You just let me know when he figures out that me being gay doesn't make us any less related."

"Theo—"

"Happy Thanksgiving, Mom."

I hung up on her. I regretted it right away, but I didn't know what else I would say if I let the conversation continue. Old feelings of anger had been stirred up at the sound of her voice, and just like that, I was reliving Halloween, drowning in the words that had latched onto my soul and hatched like maggots.

If you have a boyfriend, the least you could do is have the balls to tell me to my face like a man.

Were you like...into it, though?

Honestly.

It had taken me a full hour to calm down.

So yeah, I doubted I would be going back for Christmas. I was also uncomfortably aware of the fact that I would probably have to open up to Dominic a little about my family situation. He was bound to think it was weird if I chose to be alone again for the holidays. What should I say though?

Sorry, being alone and pathetic may sound, well, fucking pathetic, but it's actually what I prefer. I don't want to be with my parents, but I also don't want to go with you and meet your family, because that would mean...

Well, that was the problem, wasn't it? I wasn't ready to ask myself what it would mean.

My turbulent thoughts were interpreted by the sound of a text. I fished my phone out of my apron pocket and looked at the screen. Dominic wanted to know what I was doing tonight. I stepped into the back for a second so I could respond without Klyde leering at me: *I'm extremely busy with doing nothing, but I'd be happy to pencil you in.*

(Dominic)

Are we at the point in this relationship where I can start penalizing you for sass?

(Me)

I think I should get a 3-month minimum.

(Dominic)
Alright I guess I can wait it out. How do you feel about pasta?
(Me)
Well I can't speak for pasta, but I've always considered us pretty hot and heavy.
(Dominic)
Let's go to dinner then. When do you get off work? I'll pick you up.
(Me)
Six. See you then.

He sent back a smiley face. I considered sending a heart, then thought better of it. I went for a "thumbs up" emoji instead.

"I heard a barista with a great ass needed a ride," Dominic said as I climbed into the passenger seat and slammed the door.

"If one shows up, I'll be sure to let you know," I said.

"You're an adequate substitute, I guess."

He glanced at me out of the corner of his eye. His lips curved into a slow, easy smile that made me flush. I coughed and awkwardly fiddled with my seat belt as we drove down the snowy street.

"Cut it out," I grunted.

"Cut what out?"

"I feel like that piece of cheesecake."

"Don't be ridiculous, Theodore. Although if you want me to lick you, all you have to do is ask."

"Eyes on the road, Dominic."

"I'd rather have them on you."

"That's very nice, but it's snowing and people drive like morons."

He chuckled, staring through the windshield as we waited for the light to change. Then I saw his eyes go wide, and he leaned forward in his seat to squint intently out the window.

"What's wrong?" I asked.

"Nothing. Sorry." He settled back into his seat with a sigh. "That person crossing the street looked like one of my exes for a sec. I thought I might have to drive us off a cliff."

I grinned. The light changed, and he rolled slowly through it. When he turned the corner, I said:

"Do most of your exes live in the city? Should I change my routine?"

"Don't worry. Only a few of them live on this block."

"*This* block? How many do you have?"

He was silent for a bit. I felt my good mood evaporate.

Fuck. Is it so many he has to actually think about it?

"I figured out I was gay about a year ago," he said finally. "Before that there were women. I thought if I slept with enough of them, I'd eventually like it. It was a shitty thing to do. They didn't deserve that." A rush of color surged into his cheeks as he blurted: "I've actually never gone out with a man."

"Could've fooled me. You really seemed to know what you were doing when you cornered me in that alley. I felt like a flustered middle schooler."

"I sweated so much around you, Theodore."

"What?"

"We're talking major swamp-ass. I had to change when I got home."

I burst out laughing. He grinned. "Anyway, I know you've been out a while, so I guess I just assumed you had a lot of experience."

"Yeah, it'll be hard for you to measure up to awkward groping in a hallway closet. But you'll just have to do your best."

He smiled slyly. "Just groping?"

I shifted in my seat, my chest tightening with anxiety.

"Sorry," he said, reddening. "I didn't mean to pry."

"No, it's okay. It's just depressing to think about."

We stopped at another light. When I turned to look at him, Dominic suddenly reached across the console and brushed the hair away from my forehead; his cool fingertips grazed my eyelids. The contact only lasted for half a second, but I was surprised by how much comfort it brought me. The knots in my stomach shivered and then loosened. The light turned green and I clutched at my seatbelt strap again, swallowing hard as I stared at the window.

"Look, as long as we're being honest here, I should probably let you know that I—I don't really know how to..." I cleared my throat and forced myself to continue. "I've never gone very far in any of my relationships."

"That's fine."

He didn't seem to understand what I was getting at, so I struggled to clarify. "What I mean is, I won't know what I'm doing. I'll probably be really bad at...*it.*"

"Everyone is. You just take your pants off and hope for the best."

"Well that's a depressing revelation."

He snickered. I squirmed in my seat and considered keeping the next part of my worries to myself, but—-fuck it. Best to just get this over with so he could leave as soon as possible and minimize my emotional damage.

"Hey, so..."

"Mm?" He was squinting through the windshield again. I wondered if he'd spotted another ex-girlfriend already. I continued nervously.

"It's not just about me being bad at it. It's more like...I don't even know if I *want* to."

He was silent for a moment as he pulled the car up to the curb of a cute Italian restaurant; the lights hanging from the awning shifted across our windshield, glazing the glass in gold. When Dominic turned around in his seat to look at me, my breath tangled in my throat. Even though I knew our short relationship was about to end, I couldn't help but lose myself one more time in his eyes. They looked limpid and navy-blue in the darkness.

"That's fine, Theodore. I don't need that."

I blinked. There was a beat of silence as my brain struggled to grasp what he had just said to me.

"I don't believe you," I said flatly.

"Then keep me around long enough to prove it."

"But how long will that take?"

He laughed.

"Isn't that up to you?"

I stared at him from across the console for several seconds. Snowflakes scattered their powdery skins across the dark window glass behind him.

"What're you thinking?" he asked finally.

"That you're nuts and I should probably tell you to piss off. But if you want to torture yourself, I guess it's a free country."

He cocked his head to the side. "Is that your way of saying *please stay with me, Dominic*?"

I gave a non-committal grunt. He grinned and opened the car door behind him. I followed suit, thankful to have a moment to hide my face as I climbed out of the car and into the gentle snowfall.

Chapter Six: Peppermint Kiss

I invited Dominic to my place for the first time the following week. We put on lousy holiday movies and decorated a table-top tree I had stashed away in a cabinet. Dominic saw it when he was looking for a plate for his Christmas cookies (which he had baked from scratch. This man was just the gift that kept on giving.)

"Hey, let's put this up," he called from the kitchen. "Do you have any lights?"

"What?" I poked my head around the corner, half a chocolate-chip cookie hanging out of my mouth. "Oh. I forgot about that."

Dominic dragged the sad little tree out of its dark prison. His eyes were bright and his cheeks were flushed apple-red; he had such an aura of festive cheer about him that I didn't have the heart to refuse. I fished out some cheap ornaments I had shoved in a box under my bed, and we spent a few happy hours arguing about the right way to hang them up while we finished his cookies.

"Where'd you get this poor thing anyway?" he asked, arranging some lights on one of the straggly branches. "It's like the Charlie Brown tree."

"My mom got it for me when I first moved out. Guess she figured I'd be too lazy to get a real tree. She was right on the money."

"Are you close with your mom?"

I moved around the table and bent low under the pretext of looking for a place to hang up an ornament shaped like a gingerbread man. Really I just wanted an excuse to hide my face for a second.

"Not so much these days." I braced myself for follow up questions, but they never came. We decorated in silence for a moment while Jim

Carrey's *How the Grinch Stole Christmas* played on the T.V. in the background. "I haven't been home in a while," I said.

"Well, I'd like to reiterate what I said at Thanksgiving. You're always welcome to come to my parents' house—-though I know we haven't been going out for very long, so maybe that's a little weird."

"Thanks," I said, feeling warm all of a sudden. "I appreciate it, but I doubt I'd be much of an asset to the festivities."

Dominic craned his neck around the little tree. His face appeared so suddenly that I jumped, and a startled flush crept up my neck.

"Not true," he said with a grin. "My family is already embarrassingly invested in you. Especially my siblings."

"Wait, really?" I didn't add that I had yet to tell my folks about us—but that was a whole other conversation, and I didn't feel like having it right now.

"We're German Catholics, Theodore. We can't keep our lives or our opinions to ourselves."

"I didn't know you were Catholic."

"Afraid so. My parents' house has more saint devotionals than furniture."

I smiled as I adjusted a green bauble hanging crookedly on one of the branches. "Was it hard for you to come out?"

"Not really. My parents kind of knew before I did. I was pretty lucky. None of my siblings cared either."

"That's...really cool."

I bent down to pick up the now-empty box of decorations. I put it in the corner, and when I turned back around to face him, I saw that he was staring at me with a strange look on his face.

"What about you?" he asked.

I flopped onto the couch with a grunt, staring at the T.V. without really seeing it.

"My parents were weird about it."

Dominic sat down next to me, his hands folded in his lap.

"They treat me differently now," I said. I moved my gaze from the T.V. to my knees. I felt Dominic shift in his seat. The air stirred with his gentle scent.

Why do I suddenly want to cry?

And before I could even attempt to understand the strange rush of feelings brewing inside of me, I was telling him about Daniel and Halloween. As I spoke, I felt an immense pressure pass out of my body, like I was expelling dozens of iron weights. Dominic sat there and let me bluster into the void, receiving my pain and anger with all the silent tenderness of a mute nun. I didn't know how long I ranted, but when I slumped back into the cushions, I felt like I had just run a ten-mile marathon. There was a long silence. Then:

"Theodore?"

"Yeah?" I said wearily.

"Can I hold you?"

I nodded and scooted into his arms, lying my cheek against his chest. He held me against his heart for the next half hour.

I went to work early the next day. The café was slightly creepy in the bleak light of early morning. The Christmas lights Emma had strung everywhere were operating on a timer, and they weren't set to flick on until nine o'clock. The dining area was full of shadows, and the chairs and tables cast weird silhouettes on the wall. It was like I was in a room full of ghosts. I took my time cleaning the espresso machine and wiping down the tables, enjoying the silence and the shadows. It was peaceful being alone with my thoughts—which was something I never thought I'd say.

At nine-thirty Klyde came bustling in. He was carrying a box of newly ordered coffee grounds, as well as the ingredients for our seasonal menu. We had a lot of Christmas-themed drinks, but the most popular one this year was "Peppermint Kiss." It was a mint-flavored mocha topped with whipped cream, candy cane, and curls of chocolate. I thought it would taste like toothpaste and Listerine, but when I tried it, I was pleasantly surprised. The customers seemed to like it too. We'd been selling out every day—and today was no exception.

"Buy yourself something pretty," Klyde said, slapping a wad of bills into my hand at the end of my shift. "Oh, and don't forget we're closed until January 2nd."

"Yeah, I know. Merry Christmas."

"You too, man. Feel free to come by our place if you want. My Presbyterian in-laws are coming this year and we're doing a whole Hanukkah-Christmas hybrid thing. The kids will be high on sugar and fucking insane, but Emma's making cocktails so I'll be too drunk to care."

I grinned. "Thanks. Maybe I will."

"What's your boy doing?"

"Going home."

"You meet his folks yet?"

"Are you writing a fucking book or something?"

"I was hoping to squeeze a few details out of you while your guard was down."

"My guard is never down. See ya."

"Happy holidays."

I let the door slam behind me, shaking my head as I buttoned my coat and started walking to my car. It was snowing. The streets looked like they were dusted with powdered sugar, and every tree lining the sidewalk was drenched in multicolored Christmas lights. The entire block glowed. I stood on the sidewalk for a few minutes, taking in the sights and savoring the gentle brush of snowflakes on my face. The light-covered branches over my head were spindly and thin, with tufts of scraggly pine needles sprouting from their ends.

Like that tree from Charlie Brown.

"Theodore?"

The voice shattered the white silence. I turned around, annoyed at first, but then my heart leapt with surprised joy. It was Dominic. He was wearing a long black coat and a thick, burgundy scarf that made his eyes look even bluer.

"You scared me," I said, hurrying eagerly towards him. "What're you doing out here?"

"Are you okay?"

"What?"

"You didn't text me very much today. I thought it might be because of what happened yesterday. I shouldn't have pried into your family like that. I'm sorry."

He dragged his ass down here because I took longer than usual to reply to a few texts?

"We were really busy today," I said, stumbling a little through my words. I felt my cheeks growing hot. "It wasn't because I was upset or anything. I didn't mind talking about that stuff. You're a good listener."

"I am?"

"Yeah. Sorry if I worried you."

"Oh."

Dominic averted his face as a warm flush crept up the side of his neck. The snowy lights dangling from the trees threw a lush rainbow over his dark hair.

"Well then." He gave an awkward little laugh. "This doesn't make me look needy at all, does it?"

I grinned. "Yeah, it's a little Annie Wilkes, if I'm being honest."

"Never pegged you for a King fan. You seem like you have far too delicate of a constitution."

"Suck it. I'm incredibly well read."

"Then why does the majority of your vocabulary consist of the words 'fuck' and 'off'?"

"I said 'well-read,' not 'creative.'"

"See, this is the kind of top-notch banter I missed in our texts today."

"I missed you too."

As soon as the words left my mouth, I felt my insides shrivel with embarrassment. *That's not what he said, asshole!*

"I better get going," I said quickly. "But I'll text you when I get home so you know I'm not spending the night sobbing in a closet."

"You're lucky you're cute. You have an unbearable personality."

I smiled. "'Night, Dominic."

"Good night."

Neither of us moved. I could feel my throbbing heartbeat counting every second that passed. Then he took a few steps toward me. I could see the snowflakes dusting his long eyelashes. The breath from our lips steamed in the cold air and intermingled in the space between us.

"I really think I should go," I said. My voice shook.

"So go," he said softly.

The Christmas lights glowed on Dominic's glasses, blending into a dazzling kaleidoscope of color that still dulled in comparison to the blueness of his eyes. A cold gust of wind tossed powdery clouds of snow into the air; they glittered like scattered tinsel in the streetlights. When he reached down to tuck a wayward strand of hair behind my ear, the look on his face filled me with a feeling that was so sweet and warm it made me dizzy.

I love him.

Desire unfurled like a sleeping lion in my stomach. I seized his coat and pulled him closer.

Our lips touched with an urgency that took my breath away. His cold hands cupped either side of my neck, his fingers threading eagerly through my hair. At one point his glasses were sliding off his face, but he didn't even seem to notice. He only leaned harder into the kiss, causing me to stagger back a few steps as he pushed his firm, slim body against mine. I had to break away after just a few seconds; my warm, quick breath created puffs of steam between our panting lips.

"I'm sorry," he said breathlessly. "Too much?"

"N-no, it was...nice."

Jesus, listen to you, you thin-lipped ass for brains. NICE? It was only the best thirty seconds of your life.

He smiled as he straightened his foggy glasses. Then he bent down and pressed his lips to my hair, his arms encircling my shoulders.

"Good night then," he said softly. "For real this time."

My recent revelation seared through my head again, a flame of clarity in a mind that was thick with new desire.

I have to go. I really have to go. If I don't...

I felt myself sinking into him again, my throbbing body eager to keep contact.

...this will turn into something.

Dominic must have sensed my mental turmoil because I felt him gently detangling himself from our embrace. The way he was looking at me made my stomach boil. No one had ever looked at me like that before. I turned away before I could grab him again. I felt his gaze following me as I hurried down the sidewalk, but I didn't dare look back. It took me a few tries to open the car door; my hands were shaking so much I could barely grip the handle. I sat in the driver's seat for a long time, watching snow accumulate on my dark windshield.

I really love him. Shit.

I felt a sharp sting of fear lash across my heart—fear of myself and what I wanted.

Chapter Seven: Christmas Cranberries

I woke up to a snowy Christmas Eve. My apartment was on the ninth floor, affording me a spectacular view from my living room of an immaculately white city glittering like diamonds under the bright winter sun. As I staggered into the kitchen to make coffee, I heard my phone vibrate on the counter. I went over to check it and felt my stomach jump with nervous dread.

(Mom)

Merry Christmas sweetheart. Not sure what you're doing tomorrow, but feel free to swing by anytime. We'd love to see you.

I sardonically enjoyed her use of the royal *we*. Dad was hardly crying about the estrangement. What would I even say to them when I walked through the front door?

Hey Mom, Dad, still gay, hope that's not a problem? Oh wait, it is? Right, well, Merry Christmas then, guess I'll just be on my big gay way.

I stared at my phone for a solid five minutes before I sent a reply: *I might swing by. Love you.* It was a vague enough response so that it didn't commit me to anything, and it wouldn't hurt her feelings—at least I hoped not.

She's trying, I guess.

As I turned away from the counter, coffee in hand, I spotted a bottle of fancy gin sitting near my toaster. Oh yeah. I'd bought it on a whim the other day as a Christmas present for Dominic. He'd mentioned how gin was the only liquor that didn't make his stomach ache.

Though we haven't been going out long...what if he didn't get me anything? Then I've just made things weird. I should probably just—

My phone pinged. My stomach jumped again—but for a very different reason this time.

(Dominic)

Hey I'm going straight from work to my parents today, but I'd like to see you before I head out if that's okay?

(Me)

Sure. Just let me know what time works for you.

(Dominic)

Swing by my building around 5? I have a present for you too :) And don't worry. It's not another plant.

(Me)

Good. I can barely take care of Sir Percy as it is.

(Dominic)

Percy better not be your husband.

(Me)

Oh sorry that's what I named your jade plant.

(Dominic)

Heart attack avoided.

I grinned and put my phone down. My eyes wandered over to the gin bottle. I guess I'd be putting a bow on it after all.

It took about fifteen minutes for me to drive from my apartment to Dominic's workplace. I pulled up in front of a sleek corporate building, paid too much for parking like every other city dweller, and then rode the elevator up to the 6th floor.

I was buzzed into a cozy waiting room. The walls were pale blue, and there was a little fountain in the corner that instantly made me feel like I had to pee. A woman with platinum braids stood behind the front desk, gathering up her things. A gold-framed painting of a lake filled with swans hung on the wall behind her. When I gave her my name, she looked at me with an unusual amount of interest before she told me to go down the hall and through the door on the left. Then she bustled out humming Christmas carols.

I knocked on the door she pointed out, and a few seconds later it swung open and Dominic beckoned me inside. I'd never been to a massage therapist before. I was surprised by how snug it was inside the actual working space.

"I was told Mr. Evans was expecting me," I said as he shut the door behind me.

"He very much is," he said, smiling; the words were playful enough, but the way he said them made me color hotly.

"Right. Well...here." I awkwardly held out the gin.

"I'm going to have a very merry Christmas." He grinned as he examined the bottle. "Although now I'm embarrassed."

"Why?"

He went over to the massage table. There was a gift bag resting on top of it, which he picked up and handed to me. I peeked inside, then carefully pulled out a light green planter.

"I thought your jade plant might need a bigger pot eventually, and that one is the same color as your eyes, which I'm now realizing is a bit cheesy, but..." His voice trailed away with embarrassment. His face was bright red. I held the planter in both hands and felt a lump rising in my throat.

God, I must have it bad if I get all choked up over a pot.

"Thanks. You're...really sweet."

His cheeks burned even brighter. "I hope it's the right kind."

I laughed as I turned around to set the pot back down onto the massage table. "There isn't really a wrong way to buy a planter. Did I get you the right kind of gin?"

"I like whichever brand gets me the drunkest."

"Solid reasoning."

"And if you're okay with it, I'd like to open it with you when I get home."

"Shouldn't you bring it to your parents? You know. Just in case you need an emergency solution for any family drama."

He laughed as he set the gin down onto a little table in the corner right next to a pink salt lamp I hadn't noticed before.

"If I do need something extra, I'm sure my Mom will have it covered. The one thing Catholics have in abundance at every family gathering is booze."

"I don't think that's just a Catholic thing," I said, snickering as I leaned against the massage table and crossed my arms over my chest. "My parents will probably be knee deep in wine by the time I get there."

"You're going home for Christmas?"

"Maybe. I don't want to keep blowing off my mom. I think she's trying, even though it's all still pretty shitty."

"Have you talked to your dad lately?"

"Nope. I'm sure the whole visit will be a bucket of yucks. Come to think of it, maybe I'm the one who should take the gin."

"If you want it that bad, you'll just have to wait for me to come back."

"I guess I can do that."

There was a brief silence as we stared at each other. My eyes slowly traced every curve of his face, committing it to memory—which was stupid because I knew we weren't going to be apart for that long. But I already missed him.

"Don't look at me like that," Dominic said. "It makes me want to do something unprofessional."

I felt the bones in my knees soften. It was a good thing I was leaning against the massage table.

How many naked people have been on this thing today? I wonder if it would hold more than one person...wait, what the absolute fuck am I thinking right now?

There was another silence, and then Dominic closed the distance between us so fast I barely had time to take a breath. He stood in front of me, leaning forward so that his arms were on either side of my waist, his palms pressed flat against the cushy surface of the massage table. His hips were pressing into mine, and I felt an alarming mutual heat swelling between our thighs.

"That lady at the front desk might come back," I said weakly. My protest was half-hearted; I could already feel myself softening against the lines of his body.

"I gave her the afternoon off. Nobody's coming," he said with a grin that seemed to add *"for you."* He leaned forward and pressed his face against the side of my neck. "You smell wonderful."

"It's amazing what shampoo can do for a man."

"Mm. It's more than that though. Even your skin...it makes me dizzy..."

His voice trailed away as his mouth traced my jaw. The heat in my body spilled over; I heard his breath catch as my excitement stubbornly made itself known even through the thick corduroy trousers I was wearing. I felt my cheeks blaze with embarrassment. I tried to duck my face against his shoulder, but his fingers gripped my chin and he forced me to look up at him.

"Tell me what you're thinking."

Hot, tumultuous thoughts spilled in a blaze of fire across my brain: *That you're wearing too much clothing. That I want to taste every inch of you with my tongue. That I want to pin you against the wall and just—*

"I'm thinking...you look like you want to kiss me."

He smiled. "Is that what *you* want?"

"Yes," I said hoarsely. 'I'd really—-"

His mouth had already closed over my trembling lips, and the rest of my sentence dissolved into feverish panting. I clutched fistfuls of his sweater and pulled him into my quivering body. For a few minutes everything was fragrant and soft and warm; his hands moved from my hair to my waist and then slid up my back, gathering me close against his chest. I always felt so small in Dominic's arms—small and safe.

My parents lived in the suburbs. It took about twenty minutes to drive there, which was just long enough for me to consider turning around at least half a dozen times. When I pulled my car up to their house, I spent another ten minutes staring out the windshield. Finally I flung open the door and almost ran up the walk, not giving myself any more time to regret this decision. I impatiently pushed the doorbell and listened to the familiar *dong* echoing down the hall. Then the door swung open and my father was staring down at me like he couldn't believe his eyes. Which he probably couldn't. Mom had clearly neglected to mention that I might drop by. No problem. Why make this whole thing any less uncomfortable, after all?

I felt a complicated array of emotions ruffle through me at the sight of his face. I didn't look anything like him—he was a heavy, solid wall of muscle with a tan complexion, short dark hair that stuck straight up from his skull, and gray eyes—but Mom always said we both had "rubber faces." "You guys can't hide your feelings to save your life." But I was clearly better at it than she thought. After all, I had hidden my gayness for decades and neither one of them had caught on until I spelled it out for them.

"Theodore?" he said, squinting at me in the bright winter sunlight.

"Are you waiting for me to grant you three wishes, or are you gonna let me in?"

He stepped back, still staring at me like I was a zoo animal. I brushed past him and into the living room. My mother was sitting in a green armchair by the mantle, staring wistfully into the fire that was blazing in the hearth.

"Hey Mom," I said.

She looked up, startled, and then sprang to her feet. A smile of genuine delight burst across her face as she ran across the room and flung her arms around me. I had forgotten how small she was. I could have lifted her into the air with one arm.

Has it really been that long since I've hugged her?

"Theodore! Is it really you, baby? Merry Christmas! Did you hit traffic? There was an accident on the highway earlier and they had everything shut down, didn't they, Frankie?" My father had wandered into the room, his hands in his pockets and a guarded expression on his face. "Are you hungry?" Mom babbled on. "Here, come into the dining room, I've got some snacks laid out. Or do you want a drink? Dad got the stuff to make cranberry vodkas, do you still like those? Would you like one?"

"I'd like several if you're going to talk at me like this all day," I said.

There was a brief pause, and then my dad chuckled. "I'll take one too, Amy. And you should make one for yourself while you're at it."

Mom rolled her eyes at us, but she had such a big smile on her face that any irritation she might've felt got lost in translation. She bustled out of the room, leaving us alone. I went over and took her seat by the fire, sighing as I sank into the familiar velvet cushions. This thing was almost as old as I was. It had practically no springs left in the seat. Dad lumbered across the room and sat in the chair across from me—a newer one that was undoubtedly sturdier, but probably not as comfortable.

"So how've you been?" he grunted, staring into the fireplace.

Still gay, Dad.

"Okay. How're you guys?"

"Alright."

A long silence followed this chatty exchange.

God, maybe I'll just take that vodka cranberry to go and get the hell out of here.

"You still working at the coffee shop?" he asked.

"Yup."

The fire popped cheerfully. I slid further down into my chair, my hands in my pockets.

"Don't you wanna take your coat off?"

"I'm okay. Still pretty chilly."

"Don't plan on staying long?"

"Just keeping my options open," I said cautiously.

I couldn't tell if he was mad or not. My dad always had a perpetual frown line between his brows.

"Not interested in botany anymore?" he asked.

"Interest has nothing to do with it. I couldn't find any work."

"Not judgin' you, kiddo. I was just wondering—"

"—why I'm not doing things the way you want me to? Yeah, I get it, Dad. Thanks."

Another silence seeped through the room like freezing water. I was starting to feel a little queasy.

"Maybe I should just go," I said.

"Not until you've heard what I got to say."

I stared at him, and then I let out a baffled, joyless laugh. "Bye, Dad." I stood up and started to walk towards the door.

"Theodore." He stood up too. "Wait. Please."

His voice wavered. I had never heard him sound like that before. I paused, then reluctantly turned back.

"Listen, kiddo, I—"

He paused, scratched the back of his head, and then glanced towards the door like he was hoping my mother would walk in and distract us with booze. Actually, that's probably exactly what he was hoping for. Dad wasn't really known for his pep talks. I stepped on a nail when I was six years old, and when I ran to him for comfort, my face a disaster zone of tears and running snot, he said, "Walk it off, kid," without bothering to look up from his book. Yup, I could barely hold my dick straight when I peed, and here was my father telling me to shake off tetanus like a real man.

I watched him squirm for the right words, taking vicious satisfaction in knowing that he was going to dig his own grave and justify me—once again—walking out of here.

"I'm sorry, Theodore."

A punch in the ball sack would've been less startling than those words.

"What?" I said after another prolonged silence.

"For that whole thing last Halloween. I assumed the worst about you, and I wouldn't listen when you tried to tell me the truth. I wasn't even open to listening. So...I'm sorry."

"Me being with a guy is the worst thing you can think of, huh?"

"That's not what I meant."

"Well it's what you fucking said."

"I'm your father. Don't talk to me like that."

"Or what?"

The petulant response threw him off; he didn't answer, though his frown line deepened into a cavernous crevice. I went on:

"Saying you're sorry won't undo what happened, Dad. What you did sucked."

"I —"

"I know you're disappointed that I'm gay, alright? But your expectations aren't my problem and it's not fair for you to sulk about something neither one of us can control."

"Listen to me—"

"*You* listen, old man. When I came out, you didn't look me in the eye for weeks. You never asked me anything about it, or even told me you were having a hard time accepting it. You just stopped talking to me. You want me to stop swearing at you, to treat you like my father? Then start acting like it."

The crease between his brows was so deep I thought his skull might split in half. He crossed his burly arms over his chest and stared at a spot over my head for a full minute. Then he said slowly:

"Yeah, okay."

"Sorry?"

"You're right. I acted like a shithead. I have no idea how to talk to you about this and that bugs me. I get angry at myself and you, and then I get mad at your mom for some reason, probably just for good measure, and then at that point I usually open a bottle of Jack Daniel's and drink until I pass out. It looks like there's no Jack around this time, so...guess I'll have to deal with this like a grown up." A softness crept into his eyes. "I love you, kiddo. Okay? You can be gay, straight, or fucking Big Bird. Doesn't change the way I feel. That being said, I'm gonna need more time to adjust—which I know probably pisses you off and that's fair enough. I do wanna be able to support you at some point. I just don't know how."

"You can start by not looking like you're holding back a big shit during this little speech."

"I'm not a miracle worker, son. Just a dad doing his best."

"Jesus. This is your best?"

"Yeah, your mom could've done way better."

I gave him a wary look, but I went and sat back down. He did too, and we both stared into the fire until Mom bustled into the room with a tray of cranberry vodkas.

"I made you two each," she said with a sly smile.

"It's a start," Dad grunted, reaching for one of the vodkas and downing half of it in one gulp.

I took a swig of my own drink and then winced. "Did you put half a bottle in here, Mom?"

"I thought you liked it strong," she said, frowning.

"Sure, but this is like rubbing alcohol."

"I'll take it if you're afraid of turning your tummy, Cinderella," Dad said, swallowing the rest of his first drink and reaching for a second.

"Hey Mom," I said without looking at him, "did you wanna let Dad know that it's the 21st century and men are allowed to be something other than macho assholes?"

"Frankie, Theodore says—-"

"Good lord, woman, I'm sitting right here, aren't I?"

I fell silent as the two of them started arguing about whether or not he needed a hearing aid. I took another sip of my vodka cranberry.

It tasted better the second time.

Chapter Eight: The Gin Chronicles

Dominic came home from his parents on the 27th. His office, like Coffee Boys, was closed until January 2nd. I would like to say we spent this time engaged in intellectual pursuits, but the truth is way more fun: we holed out in each other's apartments and made out with such reckless abandon that my lips grew chapped beyond recognition, and I'm pretty sure Dominic's glasses were now permanently lopsided.

I was surprised that none of it made me feel anxious. Physical intimacy hadn't exactly gone well for me in the past. Maybe it was because Dominic didn't touch me like he was rushing through it or afraid of getting caught. He touched me like he had all day. We spent hours leisurely exploring each other, taking shots of Christmas gin and talking about the mundane details of our days with an enthusiasm that would've been better suited to people with way more exciting lives.

But I liked learning about his body, listening to the way it responded to my touch, filing away every shudder and goosebump and heartbeat. Dominic played with mine with equal curiosity, but there were times when he seemed hesitant. I thought I was making him uncomfortable, so for a while, I tried to cool it too.

"What'd I do?" he asked one afternoon, frowning as I extracted myself from a tumble we had taken on the couch a few minutes earlier.

"What? Nothing."

He pulled himself up into a seated position, brushing the hair from my eyes. "What's wrong, Theodore?"

I hesitated for a minute. "Am I...coming on to strong or something?"

He stared at me for several seconds. Then the corners of his mouth twitched, though I couldn't imagine what was supposed to be funny. "Not at all. Why do you ask?"

"Oh. Okay. It's just—" I faltered, throwing my eyes around the room in a desperate attempt to look nonchalant. Blood curdled in my cheeks. "Nothing. Forget I said anything. Want to watch T.V.?"

"No. I want to touch you some more."

"What?" I said, startled.

He came closer, his palm cupping the side of my face as his eyes caught me in a gaze that made my heart leap into my throat. I felt the soft curves of his warm mouth against mine; my lips tingled, and I tasted gin.

"Why does that still surprise you?" he said, laughing a little as he leaned away.

"You just haven't seemed into it lately," I muttered. "I thought I was making you uncomfortable."

He paused for a half a second. "I'm just taking it slow."

I narrowed my eyes in mock rage. "So much for me setting the pace then."

He grinned. "It's for your own good."

"Doesn't feel that way."

"Hmm. Okay then." He pushed me roughly down, pinning me against the cushions. His silky hair tumbled onto my forehead, the ends curling against my eyelids as he bent over me. I gasped when his hands slipped under my tee shirt; his fingertips grazed my stomach, invoking a constellation of goosebumps.

"What, am I going too fast now?" he murmured against my neck.

I slid my arms around his back and held him close, burying my face into his shoulder.

"You said you've never been with a guy before, but you seem pretty good at this," I mumbled.

"You're just easy to please."

He slid one of his knees between my thighs. A second later I felt my traitorous body respond with aggressive enthusiasm, and a blaze of humiliation swept across my face.

"Oh my God." I put my hands over my eyes, trying to vanish into the hot darkness. "Sorry."

"Don't be." Dominic's lips began to travel down my throat. "I get like that every time I see you." I felt something slick and warm glide briefly across my collarbone; after a minute I realized it was the tip of his tongue.

Oh God.

"Tell me what you want."

"I—don't know," I gasped, my back arching as my body writhed closer to him. Everything was a blur of heat and confusion.

Dominic smiled and suddenly leaned away. "Let me know when you figure it out."

I laid on my back for a minute, blinking up at the ceiling, disheveled and sweaty and trying to process what the hell had just happened.

"Hey." He jiggled my foot. "You okay?"

"No," I groaned.

He chuckled. "It's just that if we keep going, I know I won't be able to stop."

I sat up and for a moment we stared at each other. There was a gleam in his eyes that filled my stomach with hot and writhing knots. The scent of his skin lingered on my clothing, and when I drew in a shaky breath, I could taste him on my tongue. The air between us was thick with arousal and uncertainty. I knew one word from me was all it would take to cross the threshold into unventured territory. I swallowed, my body shaking with desire and fear, my tongue unable to articulate what I wanted. Finally I said in a tiny voice:

"Then I guess we should stop."

Dominic smiled, and I scooted closer so I could rest my head on his shoulder. We lay tangled in each other's arms for the rest of the day, dozing as the snow fell in slanting lines outside the window.

We shared another bottle of gin on New Years' Eve at Dominic's place. Someone was setting fireworks off downtown, and so we turned off all the lights in the apartment, sat on the floor with our backs against the couch, and watched through the floor-length window as the Seattle skyline bloomed into a mosaic of colors.

"I may be too drunk to drive home," I said thickly, squinting at the almost empty bottle of gin.

"I can make up the couch for you, lightweight."

"Sorry."

He laughed and emptied his shot glass. His cheeks were flushed, but he didn't look nearly as hammered as I felt right now. "It's no big deal. You shouldn't drive tonight anyway. People are idiots this time of year. 'Nother shot?"

"Fill 'er up, sweet cheeks."

A spray of gold and silver fireworks lit up the room, illuminating the glossy granite countertops and the shiny wooden floors.

"You have such a grown-up apartment," I said, looking around as he refilled my glass. My hand was a little unsteady, and as I flung the gin into my mouth, some of it escaped and dribbled down my chin. I wiped my mouth with the back of my hand.

"Don't be too impressed. My parents help with the rent."

"Really? And here I thought you were a fancy business owner rolling around in massage money like fuckin'...like fuckin' Scrooge McDuck."

He grinned, then reached over and tousled my hair. "I think I'll get you some water."

"Booooo." I slouched comfortably against the couch as I listened to him bustling around in the kitchen. He returned after only a moment.

"I don't have a filter yet, so you'll have to sober up with old fashioned tap water," he said as he knelt and handed me a glass.

"Thanks." I took a few gulps and then stared at him over the rim. "Why're you like this?"

"Hm?" He was settling down next to me again, crossing his long legs as he leaned back against the couch.

"I dunno. Nice."

"You're clearly very drunk."

There were a few moments of silence while I loudly sipped my water. Then I said matter-of-factly: "Sir Percy reminds me of you."

"Oh?"

I nodded vigorously. "It's not like he makes me think *about* you. He reminds me *of* you." To my drunk brain, this distinction seemed very important.

"How so?" Dominic asked patiently—God bless him.

"I gave up on plants for a while, but when I look at Sir Percy it's like...oh yeah, this is what it could've been the whole time."

"I see."

"Why'd you go for a jade plant, anyway?"

"I thought it was pretty. It was the same color as your eyes."

"You buy a lot of things because they remind you of my eyes."

"They're my only weakness."

I turned my head and then blinked in surprise when I realized how close he was. I could see the fireworks reflected in his twilight eyes. Then he gave a tiny sigh and leaned away. I drummed my fingers against my water cup, returning my gaze to the show outside the window. The tip of my middle finger stuck to the glass for a second, and I suddenly remembered wiping the gin from my mouth a few minutes ago. I scrambled to my feet and hurried over to the kitchen.

"Theodore?"

I turned on the faucet, pumped five piles of soap onto my hands, and began to scrub them under the streaming jet. The water grew hot and painful, but I was only at fifteen seconds and I could still feel that horrible stickiness baked into my skin.

"Theodore!"

The faucet came to a gurgling stop. I blinked, feeling like I was coming out of a deep sleep, and then looked up to see Dominic standing over me with his hand on the sink handle. "The water..." he said weakly.

I looked down at my hands. They were red and swollen. Steam was drifting up from the drain.

"Oh," I said.

"What happened? Did you cut yourself?"

"I spilled gin on my hands."

"What?"

I gave him a rueful smile. The alcohol was still buzzing in my brain, making me feel bolder than usual—and more honest. "Do you remember what you said about my hands when I told you I wanted to be a botanist?"

"I said they weren't as dirty as I thought they should be. Great pick-up line, right?"

"Right. And then I went on this whole thing about how I'm kinda uptight with germs."

"Sure," he said cautiously, clearly wondering if humoring a drunk for this long was a wise choice.

"It was a lie." I gave him a sleepy grin. "I just wanna make sure none of that stuff is on my skin. So I fuss with my hands a lot."

"What stuff?"

"The sticky gloves. Duh." I patted his cheek good naturedly. "Oh, shit, hold on. I only got to fifteen."

I turned, pulling my hand from his grip as I turned on the sink again. I made sure the faucet ran cold this time, and then I rubbed my hands together for six more seconds before I shut it off.

"There," I said, satisfied. "Twenty-one."

Dominic was looking at me like I had grown a third eye.

"Why twenty-one?" he asked slowly.

"I'm tired," I announced—and suddenly I was. Dominic smiled and then guided me to the couch with his arm around my waist. We sat down and I leaned against him, yawning.

"I'll bring you some more water in a minute," he said. "Make sure you drink it before you go to sleep, okay?"

"There you go again."

"What?"

"Being nice," I mumbled, nuzzling into his shoulder.

We sat like that for a while, listening to the crackle of the fireworks until they finally sizzled into silence.

"It reminds me of Daniel," I said thickly.

The words felt sluggish and heavy on my tongue. I didn't know if I was saying them out loud or just thinking them.

"I don't say the right things...or do the right things...I don't even like the right people." A deep, boozy darkness was creeping over my brain. "So if I can...scrub hard enough...whatever's wrong with me..."

Will just go down the drain.

The last thing I felt before sinking into warm blackness was the touch of soft lips against my hair.

I cracked open a bleary eye. It took me a second to remember where I was and why I was lying on an unfamiliar couch. I had a blanket covering my body, and as I sat up, I realized my shoes had been removed too. The blinds on the window were closed, but they were highlighted with a white glow, indicating it was broad daylight. My head was pounding.

Jesus. I've been more hungover in the last few months than I ever was in college. Need to get my shit together.

I tossed the blanket off and then winced when my fingers throbbed in protest. I stared down at my hands; they were scrubbed so raw they looked like freshly slaughtered chunks of meat. I swallowed, shame flooding my stomach as the details of last night returned to me. Maybe I could sneak out before Dominic got up. I didn't know how I would ever be able look him in the face again.

As I swung my legs over the side of the couch, I noticed a glass of water sitting on the coffee table. I grabbed it and drank it in one gulp. My throat felt like sandpaper.

Good job, shit-for-brains. God, I wish I could erase the last twelve hours—or myself, actually, yeah that's a much better idea. Let's erase my entire dumb ass from the planet, it'd do the human race loads of good. I'm surprised he didn't throw me out and leave me to sleep this off in a gutter. God, what the hell did I dump on him last night...Jesus, what DIDN'T I dump on him, come to think of it...

I heard Dominic's bedroom door open. I thought about taking a running leap out the window, but I doubted I'd get too far before he stopped me. I listened tensely to his footsteps in the hall. The bathroom door slammed, then reopened, and then there were more footsteps and—

"Morning," Dominic said, shuffling into the room with fuzzy gray slippers on his feet. His hair was sticking up at a right angle, and he was still adjusting his glasses on his face. Apparently, he wore baggy gray sweats to bed. It wasn't a terrible look. In fact, it made him look very warm and huggable.

Like you have any business even thinking that shit right now!

"Morning," I said, feeling a blaze of shame creep up my neck. "So listen—"

"It's fine."

"It's not. I acted like an ass."

"Well nobody's disputing *that*." He grinned as he came over and sat next to me on the couch. I noticed he had a green tin in his hand, and when he saw me looking, he held it up so I could get a better look at it.

"Bag Balm?" I said blankly.

"My mom used to get this stuff for us in the winter when our skin would get really dry. I always have some around. Come here."

"What?"

He cranked open the tin, scooped a quarter-size amount of yellowish ointment onto his fingertips, and began massaging it into my hand. I gasped a little as his fingers glided across my chapped skin, expertly kneading the muscles until they liquefied into puddles. The ointment soothed my cracked knuckles and calmed the stinging I felt in my palms.

"Dominic." My voice was hoarse and small. "Stop."

"Why?"

"This isn't your problem. You don't have to worry, and you don't have to tell me to stop because I already know it's—"

"I'm not telling you to stop. Keep washing your hands if you want. I'll take care of them afterwards. Now hold still."

He finished one hand and then switched to the other, the tender firmness of his fingers making me wince when they pressed on a particularly sore spot. I watched him silently, a thick lump rising in my throat.

"There," he announced, rubbing the leftover ointment into his own palms. "I'm going to make some coffee and eggs. You're having both, drunkard."

"Okay," I said, struggling to speak around the lump. "Can I help?"

"Yeah. You can sit here and sober up. I'll get you more water and some meds in a second." He kissed my forehead as he stood up and made his way to the kitchen. "Happy New Year, by the way."

"At the rate I'm going, I doubt I'll last another," I mumbled.

He's still here.

"That cheerful outlook of yours is what keeps me coming back for more."

"Glad I amuse you."

He hasn't left.

"You certainly do. Oh, crap..."

"Did you just see your reflection?"

"No, your future. Spoiler alert: you're newly single."

"Fair enough."

He grinned. "I actually just realized that all I have is hazelnut coffee. Is that okay?"

"Yeah, that's fine."

I think...he's it for me.

"You take a little cream, right?"

"Yeah."

I peered over the couch and watched him prepare our breakfast. My hands still felt warm and soft from the Bag Balm.

I hope I can tell him that some day.

Chapter Nine: An Unexpected Latte

"Happy New Year," Klyde said when I walked into work on January 2nd. There were bags under his eyes and he looked like he hadn't shaved in a hot minute.

I shrugged off my coat and hung it up on the coat rack. "You still look hungover. Can't hold your booze anymore, old man?"

"I made the mistake of challenging my wife to several drinking games over the holidays. I'm going to need a full month to recover."

"*Emma* drank you under the table? I once saw her get blown over by a pleasant spring breeze."

"What can I tell you? She's a gorgeous freak. Then the kids got into some sugar because we were both too drunk to pay attention and they've bouncing off the walls for three days straight. So that's been fun."

"Wow. Dad of the year."

"I try. What about you? Do anything exciting?"

"Spent the night at Dominic's. Where's the broom? There's all this crispy shit on the floor over here."

"Sorry. I spilled some graham crackers a few minutes ago. I thought I got it all. So. What were the sleeping arrangements at this little gathering of yours? Did you allow the gentleman to keep his honor?"

"I'm going to shove this broom so far up at your ass you'll be walking like a duck for the rest of your life."

"You're so sour. And such a lovely shade of red."

I gave him a salute with both middle fingers. He went into the back, snickering, and started to stock the desserts behind the display case while I finished wiping down the tables. I was a little more careful than usual about getting any sticky residue from the rag onto my hands.

It was a pretty busy morning. I got to deal with the public's finest individuals, including a group of disgruntled men in suits who forgot where the line started; a teenage girl who changed her flavor shot five different times during her order; and a group of giggling women who still seemed drunk from the holidays. Their order was predictably stupid and complicated. By the time I finished dealing with them, I had no energy left to hoist a fake smile on my face for the next person in line: a rail-thin woman wearing black gloves, a stylish gray coat, and long gold earrings. Her sleep cap of brown hair brushed the tops of her shoulders, and rich brown eyes glittered out from behind sharp, square bangs.

"What can I get you?" I said through gritted teeth.

"Large latte, please."

"Seven sixty-three."

Her voice sounded strangely familiar. Our eyes met when I reached out to take her credit card, and something stirred in the depths of my memory. I jumped when she suddenly slapped the countertop with her palm. A grin exploded across her red, lipsticked mouth.

"Theodore Brooks!" It was like an accusation.

I stared at her for a few more seconds. Then it clicked. "Professor Wendell?"

"Ha! I knew it! It's been a while! How've you been?"

"Living the dream." I turned away to make her latte.

"Hey, gotta pay the bills, right? I'm working part-time at a grocery store these days."

"Did the university cut back your hours?"

"No, I just charge too much to my credit cards." She laughed. "So what have you been up to? You still looking for work in botany?"

"I guess. It's hard finding anything steady," I said, trying not to heave a sigh over the tired words. I was so sick of explaining this to people who were unable to grasp the fact that not everyone gets to live the life they want.

"I still use your senior thesis as an example of the kind of paper I'm looking for when I'm talking to my freshmen. Don't tell anyone, but you were one of my best students. You actually cared about the material, which is quite rare in my profession."

I grinned as I turned back around and held out her latte. "Well, I had an okay teacher."

"I'm flattered." She took her drink, hoisting her purse up onto her shoulder. "I need to run to my next class, but let me know if you're ever interested in exploring your options. I need someone competent to lead my interns in our field study this summer."

"What?" I was taken aback. "Really?"

"It wouldn't pay much—probably no more than you get here, to be honest—but it's some experience. It would look good on your resume, especially if you want to ease into a more hands-on field. Do you still have my email? Shoot me a line if you're interested."

"Thanks, Professor. I might take you up on that."

"Take care."

I watched her hurry out of the cafe in a flurry of clicking boots. When I got home later, I decided to at least check out the program she was referring to, so I cranked open my grandpa of a laptop and emailed Wendell for the details. To my surprise, she got back to me in a couple hours and I was able to see for myself what I'd be signing up for.

Honestly it looked pretty decent. The pay was definitely shit, but I'd be doing something I actually liked. It was almost too convenient though. This wasn't the first time a promising opportunity had come up over the years; they always fell through at the last minute. Did I really want to go through that again? Last time I lost a good job, I'd spent three days drinking and napping in the bathtub in my underwear.

I glanced over at my plants in the corner. "Well, ladies and gentlemen, what do we think?" I said. "Should I go for it?" They all resumed the usual dignified silence. My gaze fell on Sir Percy. The tips of his waxy leaves were growing more tinged with scarlet every day; I'd have to transfer him to Dominic's pot soon. I stared at my computer monitor for a few minutes, then took a deep breath and tapped out an email to Wendell, telling her I wanted the job and asking what further steps needed to be taken.

A week later my boyfriend met my parents. The day started out so nicely, too.

I woke up next to Dominic. We'd spent half the night smoking weed and watching 1980s comedies on the shitty T.V. I had in my bedroom. I quickly discovered that Dominic couldn't handle Mary Jane. A few puffs in and he became giggly, then handsy, then both before he collapsed against my pillows snoring. I made a mental note to always keep some weed on hand in our future. I then proceeded to smoke the rest of my own allotted portion, laughing stupidly to myself as the movies played before passing out next to him at around three in the morning. Next thing I knew I was blinking in the sun, and his beautiful face was only a few inches away from my own. Alarmed, I checked to make sure I still had my pants on. When I discovered that I did, I experienced an unexpected rush of disappointment.

"How are we feeling this morning, weed king?" I said when he cracked open a bleary eye and stared at me for several seconds.

"I have a memory of naming certain parts of your body after Disney characters, but I'm hoping to God it was all a dream."

"Why would you take that away from me, Dominic?"

"Sorry," he said, flushing.

"Do I look like I need a fucking apology, darling?"

"No, but you do smell like you need a fucking breath mint, sweetheart."

I took a cheap shot at his head with my fist, but he rolled away with a grin. I was still detangling myself from the bed sheets when my doorbell rang. Frowning, I hurried out of the bedroom and over to the buzzer near my front door.

"Yes?"

"Theodore, honey, will you buzz us into the building? It's Mom and Dad."

I felt like I'd fallen down three flights of stairs and then face-planted into a platform of concrete.

"What are you guys doing here this early?" I stammered.

"Early? It's noon—Frankie, did you hear that?"

"Yeah, it was a riot. Kiddo, as much as I'd love to stand out here all day like a jackass—"

"Uh, yeah, okay," I said, and I buzzed them in. Ten seconds later I turned around and made a beeline for the bathroom, where I could hear the sink splashing. They had to ride the elevator up nine floors and then walk to the end of the hall where my door was. I had about two minutes—if I was lucky.

"Jesus!" Dominic yelled when I kicked open the bathroom door; it ricocheted off the wall with a loud bang. "Knock much, Brooks? What if I'd been taking a dump?"

"My parents are on their way up."

"What?"

"They just showed up. They'll be at the door any second. Do I sound like I'm panicking? Because I'm fucking panicking!"

"Relax, Theodore."

"Oh my God, you're telling me to—you know that—oh shitshitshit—"

"Theodore." He put his hands on my shoulders and bent his knees so he could look me in the eyes. I grew a little calmer. A *little*. "Panicking won't make them go home. I'll smooth my hair down so they don't get any ideas—" he smiled and squeezed my shoulders—"and I'll say a very polite hello and then I'll be out of here."

"You think *you're* the problem?"

"Well, you did say they don't know about us yet."

"I don't need to hide you like a dirty magazine. *Jesus*. I'm worried they're going to be super weird around you—or rude. Honestly my dad is a wild card right now. We haven't spoken since Christmas and—"

The doorbell buzzed. I stared hopelessly at Dominic, who kissed me on the forehead and then turned me around and shoved me out of the bathroom.

"Remember to breathe."

I braced myself as I opened the front door. My parents were standing on the welcome mat. They were both carrying boxes. "Are you moving in or something?" I asked, stepping aside to let them in.

"We stopped by a nursery and your mom bought every goddamned weed there," Dad grunted, setting his box down onto the floor and then stretching his back, wincing. "That one's for you."

"What?" I stared down at the leafy growth sprouting over the rim of the cardboard.

"I thought you might like some greenery for your place," Mom said brightly, looking around my apartment. Her eyes fell on the plant corner. "I see you already have a few friends though. But we —" She stopped when there was a small noise in the bathroom. She glanced down the hall. "Oh, I'm sorry, do you have a friend over?"

My stomach was churning nervously. "That's my...boyfriend. You can meet him if you want. But if that makes you feel weird, you should leave before he comes back out."

What followed was one of the longest seconds of my life. Dad had paused mid-stretch and was looking like someone was pranking him. Mom stared at me, then at Dad, then back at me. Then she smiled.

"What's his name?"

"Dominic."

"And what does he do?"

I was taken aback by the follow up question, since I'd expected the next words out of her mouth to be: "We're leaving."

"He's a massage therapist."

"Lemmie ask you something," Dad grunted. "Why would people pay a stranger to rub them? Is it a sex thing?"

"For God's sake, Frankie, he's not talking about that kind of massage. Are you?" Mom shot me a nervous look.

"No, Mother. Dominic does not jerk people off for cash."

"See, Frankie? It's for therapy, right, dear? Professional athletes get them all the time. It keeps them limber. You really should consider getting one yourself sometime, Frankie. You're so tightly wound you can barely walk straight."

The bathroom door opened and Dominic came around the corner. All three of us looked at him in a single, fluid, inadvertently well-coordinated movement that I'm sure made him feel like he was starring in his own horror movie. He'd done a good job cleaning himself up. He looked fresh out of the oven, rather than what he really was: sloppy leftovers from a night of weed and 80s movies. Dad shocked me by stepping forward with his hand held out.

"Hey there. I'm Frank Brooks."

Dominic shook it.

"Dominic Evans. It's nice to meet you."

My mother was determined not to be left out. She elbowed her husband out of the way as she eagerly jumped forward and took Dominic's still-extended hand.

"I'm Theodore's Mom, Amy. It's so nice to meet you, Dominic. Where are you from? Any siblings? How long have you been practicing massage therapy?"

"Seattle, six, and a couple years," Dominic said soberly. He glanced at me out of the corner of his eye. I saw his lips twitch.

"You should help Theodore arrange some of these plants," Mom went on. "We got them at the place on East Pine Street. Have you ever been there before? It's a lovely little store."

"That's where I bought this one, actually."

"Oh, is that a jade plant? Theodore, didn't you have something like this when you were little?"

"Possibly. I've killed many plants in my time."

They wandered over to the plant corner, chatting it up like they were old friends. Dad crossed his arms and scowled.

"He doesn't *look* gay."

"All part of the big gay agenda, Dad. You'll never see us coming."

He raised his eyebrows at me, but the side of his mouth turned up into a small smile. "Sorry, I didn't mean it like that. I knew a few fellas back when I was a kid and they were always—obvious, you know? Like the way they talked and moved. This kid looks nor—nice." He averted his gaze for a second, the back of his neck turning red.

"Want a drink?" I said grimly. "I have whiskey or, if you prefer, a bottle of NyQuil."

"I'll start with the whiskey," he grunted.

So I sat down and had a drink with my dad in my apartment—something I hadn't done in years. Then my mother and boyfriend came over and had a drink with us, and I found myself wondering why this hadn't blown up in my face yet. We spent a solid twenty minutes acting like a civilized group of homo sapiens before Dad started to gripe about the parking meters.

"We'd better head out before he starts throwing things," Mom said, laughing as she wrapped me in a hug. "Take care of those plants, okay?"

"Sure. Thanks."

My dad shook hands with Dominic again—I knew he was testing the firmness, as he'd always told me you could "tell a lot about a man from his handshake"—and then they were gone. The door clicked behind them. I stood there in stunned silence for a few minutes while Dominic cleaned up the empty whiskey glasses. Finally I picked my jaw up from the floor and I turned my attention to the box of plants still sitting on the floor. I transferred it to the dining room table and began to sort through them.

"That one looks like a Mr. Darcy," Dominic asked, flopping into the chair across from me.

"This?" I held up an Inchplant, its purple tendrils dangling over a chubby ceramic pot. "Looks more like a Miss Bingley to me."

He smiled. "So are you okay?"

"Yeah, it's fine. They had to meet you eventually."

"Do they drop by like that a lot?"

"No, this was definitely weird." I set aside Miss Bingley and pulled out the next one: a scraggly pothos plant.

"Don't you already have one like that?" Dominic asked.

"Yeah, they're common house plants because they're so hardy. I like the way the leaves are shaped on this one. I bet I could coax it to grow up the window, get a cool vine curtain thing going...what're you looking at?"

"I can't look at you?"

"Not like that."

He leaned forward on his elbows, glancing up at me through his eyelashes. "I just think you're cute."

"Keep it in your pants, Evans."

"I'm doing my best," he said with a little laugh. I looked at him for a moment. I felt my ears growing warm. "What?" he asked.

"I've been wondering something."

"Shoot."

"You said before that we didn't have to have sex, but do you think you'd ever want to?"

Dominic sat up straight in his seat and frowned at me for a moment. He had a habit of biting down on his lower lip when he was thinking. It was very distracting.

"I think so," he said finally.

"Not really the enthusiastic 'yes' I was hoping for."

He laughed. "What I meant was that I'm definitely interested, but since I've never been with a man, I'm not really sure how to...do it right." He flushed.

"That's okay. I looked some stuff up."

I went over to the coffee table, picked up the notebook I'd been scribbling in over the last few days, and then back over to the dining room table and slapped it down in front of him. Dominic stared at it.

"You seem pretty organized for someone who's supposedly as green as I am."

"I just like being prepared."

He took a few minutes to flip through the notebook. Then he leaned back in his seat, crossing his arms over his chest. I suddenly felt like I was in a corporate meeting, negotiating a crucial business deal.

"Okay, full disclosure?" he said.

"Yup."

"Most of what you have in there terrifies me."

"Good, me too."

"Then why...?"

"I just figured you should have the same information I do," I said, feeling the heat in my ears extend to my cheeks.

"I appreciate that," he said. He looked relieved. "So...how would you like it to go? Anything off the table?"

"I don't want to be—um—" Like a fifth grader, I made a circle with my thumb and pointer finger and then awkwardly poked through the hole with my opposite pointer finger. Dominic burst out laughing. "I don't wanna say it!" I snapped, mortified.

"I haven't seen someone do that since middle school. Don't worry, though. Me neither."

"I thought one person had to do it."

"I don't think anyone *has* to do anything," he said, smiling. "I don't want us to force it, Theodore. I'd just like to..." He stopped, then nervously scratched the back of his neck. "I just want to be with you, however that looks."

"Me too," I said, slipping my hands in my pockets so he couldn't see them shaking. "So...what about you? Anything I should know? What do you like?"

"You."

"Quit taking cheap shots and answer the question."

He grinned. "Can I think about a few options and get back to you?"

"Yeah, of course."

There was a pause. All the sex talk had me worked up, and just when I'd decided to take my new green friends over to the plant corner to distract myself, Dominic stood up and walked around the table towards me. I instinctively took a few steps back.

"Don't try to run," he said. "We both know I'm faster."

"Is that a proven fact?" I said, continuing to back away even as he easily closed the distance between us with his long legs. "Easy, Evans. I wasn't thinking I wanted to do anything right *now*—"

"Oh, I'll behave myself as far as *that's* concerned. But we're definitely doing something."

I staggered back a few more steps until I hit the wall behind me.

"Nowhere left to go," he said quietly, towering over me. "God, your eyes do things to me I never saw coming."

He took me in his arms before I could even pretend to play hard to get.

Chapter Ten: Lover's Delight

Valentine's Day was always busy for Coffee Boys. Everyone and their mother seemed to choose the café as a date spot, and I spent the majority of my shift catering to happy—and not so happy—couples trying desperately to impress one another. Klyde created a special drink for the day called "Lover's Delight." It was a confection of vanilla flavored coffee with pink, heart-shaped candy sprinkled on top of mounds of whipped cream. It wasn't his most creative work, but since people liked to buy festive drinks, it sold out by the end of the day.

"You're a charlatan," I said as we were locking up the café for the evening. "This is just a vanilla latte with pink shit on top and people pay twice as much for it."

"You have no artistic eye."

"But I do have actual eyes, and anyone can see your Lover's Delight is just crap in a cup."

"Speaking of lovers, you got any plans with the boy toy today?"

"Fuck off."

"That would be a yes, then."

I pulled off my hideous yellow apron and threw it at him. "Do me a favor and wrap this around your head until you stop breathing."

"Rude. Think of my wife and children."

"They'd be better off without you."

"I thought having a boyfriend would make you nicer," Klyde pouted as he bent down to lock up the display case under the counter. "Love is supposed to make you sweeter."

"Does it? Having a wife doesn't seem to have done much for your annoying personality, old man."

"Oh-ho, so you *are* in love, then?"

"I'll see you tomorrow," I said, glaring at him as I walked towards the front door.

"Your heart is on your face," he called after me, grinning.

"There's nothing on your face but a moronic expression."

"Don't be—"

I slammed the door, cutting off the rest of his sentence. I buttoned up my coat as I hurried to my car. Dominic was going to come to my apartment later. We'd promised to have dinner together and I was supposed to be in charge of the salad—which you'd think would be a hard dish to ruin, but I knew I'd find a way if I wasn't careful. I checked my phone as I got into my car. I had forty minutes until he showed up, which was just enough time to navigate traffic, yell at assholes who cut me off on the road, get back to my place, and throw some leafy greens into a bowl.

It wasn't an elegant plan, but it was an efficient one. I got home with plenty of time to spare, and I had just finished setting the table when I heard him knock on the door.

"I'm embarrassed at my contribution to this date," I said, watching him set a crockpot of roast and potatoes down onto the table.

"You shouldn't be. We're growing boys, after all. We need our veggies."

"Not sure if iceberg lettuce counts...oh wait, I have wine. That should increase my relationship stock, right?"

"Significantly."

I limited myself to one glass with dinner—which wasn't too hard since it was a Moscato. I liked dry wines but I knew Dominic preferred sweeter vintages, and so I had deliberately chosen one I knew he would enjoy. Plus, I figured it wouldn't tempt me to over-indulge. Our relationship had already survived one drunken episode; I had no intention of testing it with another.

"You sure you don't wanna help me drink more of this?" Dominic asked when we were sitting on the couch after dinner, digesting our meal. He held up a half-empty bottle.

"It's all yours."

"Are you trying to get me drunk?"

"Not deliberately, but if it happens, I willingly surrender myself to whatever advances you may make."

He grinned and poured himself another glass.

"You're hand isn't even steady, you lush," I said, laughing as I reached up to steady the bottle for him. Wine slopped into his glass, splashing over the rim. A few drops got on one of my fingers.

"Wups," he said. "Sorry."

Before I could even process what happened, Dominic had set his cup down, lifted my hand, and slipped my finger into his mouth. For an endless second, the only thing that seemed to exist was the gentle sucking of his lips and the silky brush of his tongue against my skin.

"There," he said quietly, once he had finished. He was looking at me from over my knuckles with an expression in his eyes that made my brain malfunction. "All clean."

I swallowed. "There was nothing clean about that, sir."

He smiled and kissed the back of my hand before releasing it. "Let me know if you still feel sticky later."

I felt myself reddening, which only made his smile widen. We sat side by side on the couch, watching whatever romcoms were playing on cable, until Dominic checked his phone and realized it was much later than either of us had thought.

"It's coming down pretty bad," I said, glancing out the window at the snowfall.

"I didn't know it was supposed to last this long," Dominic said, frowning as he followed my gaze.

"Did you want to crash here tonight?" I asked. "The roads are probably lousy. Besides, I'd like to return the favor for when you put up with my drunk ass on New Year's Eve."

"You sure you don't mind?"

"It's no problem." I went down the hall to the linen closet and got him a few blankets. When I came back out, he was already lying on the couch, dozing. He jumped a little when I put a quilt over him. "Feel free to get more blankets from the closet if you need them, okay? It gets cold in here at night."

When I began to lean away, his hands suddenly gripped the back of my neck and pulled me down for a kiss that felt more like we were starting something than saying goodnight.

"Thanks," he said, his eyes already fluttering shut. "Good night, Theodore."

"Night."

I hurried off to my own bedroom, feeling breathless. I shut off the lights, scurried under my covers, and waited for oblivion to carry me away from the lingering impression of his kiss. But the hours ticked by, and the knowledge that Dominic was only a few steps outside my door made me feel restless and hot. I kept pressing my finger against my lips, shivering when I thought about how it had felt in his mouth. I wondered what other parts of my body he might enjoy tasting.

Shit.

I tossed and turned, kicking my blankets off, then pulling them back on, then flinging them aside again. I could feel myself shaking as something warm and primal took hold of me. After a few seconds of deliberation, I climbed out of bed, opened my door, and walked into the living room to do what I realized I had planned on doing from the moment I suggested he sleep over.

It took a few seconds for my eyes to adjust to the darkness. The couch was empty.

"Theodore?"

"Jesus!" I gasped, whipping around. Dominic was standing at the kitchen sink.

"Sorry. I got up for a glass of water. Are you okay? What're you doing out here?"

My mind jammed. It was too dark to see him clearly, but it was obvious he was waiting for me to explain myself.

"Will you...come to bed with me?"

"Sure. Are you cold? Do you want me to grab another blanket from the closet?"

"No, I mean..." I felt coils of heat spinning in my stomach. I took a deep breath and squared my shoulders. "I'd like you to come to bed, but I don't want us to sleep at all."

There was a pregnant pause. The kitchen was dark, but I could make out the silhouette of his body and the whiteness of his tee shirt looming over the kitchen sink. When he spoke, his voice was very quiet.

"You know what you're saying, right?"

"Yes," I said, not bothering to conceal the desire and desperation in my voice. "I'm saying I want to take you to my room and do things to you that I've never even considered doing before. Are you going to let me, or do you want me to beg for it?"

The moon burst through the clouds outside the window. Pale light flooded the room, and I saw the answer on his face as he came swiftly towards me. The force of his embrace almost lifted me off my feet; my back slammed into the wall behind us. For a few blazing seconds, the only thing I knew was the taste of his lips and tongue, his fingers tangling in my hair, and the sound of my own heart pounding thickly in my ears. At some point, I dimly registered that we had stumbled out of the hallway and into my bedroom. I heard the door slam, but I didn't remember touching it. Maybe Dominic kicked it shut. When the thick mists of arousal cleared for just a moment, I realized that we had fallen back onto the bed and his hands were groping my hot flesh, gliding across the contours of my bare chest and sliding up the curve of my spine. He held me so close, his panting mouth on my face and neck, and I knew nothing but the darkness and the sweet smell of his skin and hair. I wrapped my trembling legs around his waist and I pulled him to me with a desperation that would've embarrassed me if I'd been capable of feeling anything other than raw, aching need.

"Theodore," he said hoarsely; I could feel his body trembling in my arms. "Before we go any further, I need to tell you something." He pulled away for a moment so he could look me in the eyes. "I'm in love with you, and if we do this, you'll never get rid of me. Are you okay with that?"

I stared up at him, struggling to catch my breath. His body felt so warm and soft on top of mine. His cheeks and neck were flushed, his eyelashes trembling as he looked down at me with nervous anticipation.

"Yes," I whispered. He caught me in a kiss that ripped the air from my throat.

I clawed at his clothing, but I was clumsy and I didn't get very far. Dominic's hand gently closed around mine and I felt him guide my fingers until we lifted his tee shirt over his head and tossed it into the corner. Then he took off mine—very slowly and gently, like he was giving me time to reconsider. When I offered no resistance—I don't think I was even capable of putting on the brakes at this point—he took off everything else and started kissing every inch of my quivering body. The room filled with the sounds of our heavy breathing as our caresses grew longer and more intimate. My body fell into a natural rhythm against his, opening and softening in a way I had never experienced before.

"I love you," he breathed, leaning over me until the only thing within my line of vision was his blue eyes.

My answer came out hoarse and broken. "I love you too."

It was all we could say to each other the rest of the night, moaning the words in the warm darkness as silver bars of moonlight crept across the carpet.

When I opened my eyes the next morning, the first thing I noticed was how every inch of my body ached. My muscles groaned in protest as I raised myself up on my arms and squinted around the room. Then I looked down at Dominic. He was sleeping soundly next to me, his eyelashes spread out like tiny silk fans against his warm brown skin, his disheveled hair glowing chestnut in the sunlight filtering through the bedroom window. His lips were slightly open, and I could hear the gentle sound of his breathing. I stared at him for a while, wondering how someone could look this good after such a torrid night of shameless indulgence. At one point during last night's activities, I had reached such a peak of blind pleasure that I saw constellations.

His eyes fluttered open. I panicked and seized the covers, dragging them up to my chest like a startled 1950s virgin on her wedding night. As soon as I did it, I realized how stupid it was. It looked like I'd been sitting here playing myself while watching him sleep.

"Hi," Dominic said, rubbing his eyes with a knuckle. "You don't look like you slept very well."

"I didn't." I flopped down onto my back with a sigh, then turned my head to look at him. "It's all your fault."

He smiled as he leaned forward to kiss the tip of my nose. When he pulled away, I noticed several long scratches on his shoulder.

"What's that?"

"Don't worry about it."

"Did I do that?" I asked, paling. "You're bleeding!"

"I'm not. Well, not anymore."

"*Any—*"

"Theodore, stop." He dropped a gentle kiss on my cheek. "I'm fine." His eyes drifted over my face, and then he snickered. "You have really bad bed head. It's cute."

"Love really is blind."

"Not entirely. I did want to throw you out the window last night. For such a small man, you're a very rough sleeper. You kept kicking me."

"That's because you splay like a starfish and take over the whole bed."

"Is that so? I'll weigh myself down with a few more blankets next time."

"Next time?"

He came towards me with a smile that melted my bones. "Surely you didn't think this was going to be a one off."

"No, I just—" I broke off with a gasp when I felt his lips traveling down my stomach. "What're you doing?"

"Making up for taking over the bed last night." His head had vanished beneath the covers. "When do you have to go to work?"

"Not until noon." I felt him pause, his breath warm against my skin. I realized I was gripping the sides of his head, crushing handfuls of his hair between my fists. "You don't have to," I said hoarsely.

"I know. But I want to. Desperately."

His tongue flicked against my hip bone. I gnashed my teeth to prevent myself from moaning. I felt my back arch desperately towards him, pushing myself closer to his eager mouth. There was a throbbing heartbeat of silence, and then I felt Dominic start to pull away.

"No," I said weakly, tightening my grip on his hair. "Don't stop."

I knew it was a mistake to allow such things when I needed the energy to work later. Then I felt Dominic gently caress the inside of my thighs and I ceased to think at all. Hell with it. Who needed a job anyway?

Money was overrated.

"Honey, take notes," Klyde said when I bustled into work, breathless and red-faced. "This is the last day Theodore will ever work here."

"Yeah, I can always be placed by all the other employees you have—oh, wait."

"He's got you there, sweetie," Emma said with a grin. She was behind the counter, helping Klyde load some clean mugs onto a tray.

"You made my wife work, jackass," Klyde said. "Does a woman like this look like she's made for hard labor?"

"A woman like that shouldn't be with a troll like you in the first place," I said, rolling my eyes as I tied my apron around my waist. "What do you need me to do?"

"No apology for being late?"

"I'm sorry for being late, Mr. DePaul."

"That didn't sound very sincere."

"Theodore, do you want some coffee?" Emma asked. "You don't look fully awake yet."

"That'd be great, thanks."

"Are you two ignoring me?" Klyde whined.

"Sometimes it's the only way to handle you," his wife said coolly, pouring me a cup and handing it to me across the counter.

"I love it when you scold me, Emma. Wanna go in the back and scold me some more?"

"God," I groaned, shaking my head. "It's way too early for this."

Emma winked at her husband and gave a little jiggle of her hips as she crossed the room to carry a customer their order. Klyde watched her go, tilting his head and grinning at her rear end.

It was a busy day, and Emma ended up staying to help out. It was nice to have some extra hands because I couldn't stop thinking about last night. I kept reliving ever detail in my mind. God, all I wanted to do was crawl back into bed with him and never resurface.

"Thanks for picking up my slack today," I told Emma when she came into the kitchen at the end of the day, carrying a tray of dirty cups. She smiled as she brought them over to Klyde, who was standing at the sink. He was elbow-deep in dirty suds. The dishwasher had fizzled out last night and his cheap ass had yet to call a repairman.

"No problem. I like keeping an eye on him every now and then," she said, nodding towards her husband. "I'll finish cleaning up the tables and then I'll leave the rest to you boys."

"Sounds good."

She went back out onto the main floor. I got out the broom and started to sweep around the supply shelves.

"What's that?" Klyde said suddenly.

"What?"

"That song you were humming just now."

"I was humming? Sorry, I didn't notice."

Klyde looked at me for a moment, his lips pursed. Then he pointed a soapy finger at me and said flatly:

"You got some."

I looked up from my sweeping, startled. I was still staring at him when Emma walked back into the room, carrying another tray of mugs.

"Here's the last of them."

"Honey, guess what?" Klyde said, wiping imaginary tears from his eyes. "Our boy here got his cherry popped. Wait, is that right? Do you guys call it that? I guess it'd be more accurate to say taming the sna—"

I shoved my elbow into his solar plexus with as much force as I could muster. He staggered, swearing, into a pile of boxes.

"Was it the professor?" Emma asked eagerly.

"He's a massage therapist, and that's not the point here!" I snapped.

"Oooh, that's even better. Did you guys start with that, or...?"

"Yeah, what did he massage, buddy?" Klyde wheezed from the corner.

"You can both go straight to hell."

"I'm sure you'll be able to give us the grand tour," Klyde said. "We're Jewish and you're gay, so I mean, it's inevitable."

"To be fair, honey, the Chosen People still have a fighting chance," Emma said, "and as long as Theodore is an *abstinent* gay man..."

"Well that ship sailed pretty hard, didn't it, sweetie? In fact it sank right to the bottom of gay ocean."

"With great enthusiasm, it seems."

"Shitheads." I stalked out of the room. I could hear them cackling. Then, seized with a sudden impish impulse, I ducked my head back into the kitchen and said: "And I got way more than 'some.'"

Their laughter followed me out onto the main floor, where I proceeded to stack chairs against the wall with a stupid grin on my face.

Chapter Eleven: Sweet Treats and Promises

From: Elena Wendell <e.wendell@university.edu>
Mon 2/20 9:43 AM
To: Theodore Brooks <tbrooks95@gmail.com>

Hey Theodore,

Thanks for filling out the applicable paperwork. I finally managed to get the signed approval from the department supervisors (attached here for your records as well). Congrats! You're officially part of the team. I look forward to working with you this summer.

I'm not great at checking email, so if you have any questions in the meantime, feel free to give me a call at the previously specified number.

Best,

Prof. Wendell

The morning sun showered buttery squares across my rickety dining room table. The sky outside the window was the hard white blue of winter, and I could feel freezing air oozing in through the drafty window behind me. I shivered as I stared at my laptop screen for a solid five minutes. I was still staring when I heard the front door open. A second later Dominic came around the corner. He was all bundled up, wearing his usual burgundy scarf and a matching hat. God, his eyes were blue.

"Well look who it is," I said grimly. "I felt like a jilted housewife this morning."

He smiled as he dropped a kiss on top of my head and set a steaming Styrofoam mug in front of me.

"I didn't want to wake you. You were out of coffee so I went out to get some."

"Oh yeah. Shit, sorry."

"Is this an adequate excuse for my absence?"

I sipped tentatively at my drink. "I'll let it slide."

"Are you okay?" he asked as he shrugged off his coat and slid into the chair next to me. "You look grumpier than usual."

I flipped my laptop around so he could see Wendell's email. "I just got this."

He took a second to read it, and then glanced up at me.

"Isn't this good?"

"I didn't actually expect it to happen."

"Are you still interested in the job?"

I nodded, scowling at the email without really seeing the words anymore. "It's just...I haven't had a botany job in years."

What if I don't remember anything? What if the team is a bunch of little freshman shits who won't listen to me and I end up looking stupid? What if Wendell regrets hiring me and my dad gets disappointed again and Dominic leaves me—whoa, easy, you're spiraling just a teensy bit there captain—

"Doing something new is always nerve-wracking. But sometimes it really pays off." He smiled knowingly into my eyes.

"Only 'sometimes'?" I said, grinning.

He scooted his chair closer and slipped his arm around my waist. "Have I ever told you what pretty skin you have? Like roses and snow...and it's so smooth." He brushed his nose against my forehead, then started to gently kiss down the ridge of my nose. The familiar heat began to creep across my skin.

"Your hands are cold," I said, laughing as I twisted away from his caress. His hands had somehow found their way up my shirt.

"A good boyfriend would warm them up for me."

"Yeah, a good one might."

Dominic sighed. "Dating you is like breaking in a wild horse."

He tackled me to the ground before I could register what was happening, pushing me onto the carpet and then straddling my hips so he could slip his hands beneath my sweatshirt. He pressed his cold fingers against my chest, grinning as I gasped and wiggled.

"How do you stay so warm?" he asked.

"Is this your idea of setting the mood?"

"What, no good?" He bent towards me and the rest of my blustery response was lost in his kiss. I went slack against him, bombarded by sensations that turned my body into soft butter.

"How about now?" he murmured, his mouth tickling my lower lip as his teeth dragged gently down my chin.

"N-Not even close."

"Really? You feel pretty close to me."

He ran his hands through my hair as his kisses became longer and more passionate. My body was reaching the pinnacles of an excitement from which I was unlikely to ever recover. I felt like it was going to cripple me.

"Not here, Dominic." My voice was ragged with arousal. "Take me to bed."

Without another word, he swept me into his arms and carried me to the bedroom.

The first thing I did when I went into Coffee Boys the next morning was tell Klyde about my summer job.

"Great. What am I supposed to do now, hire college kids?" he scoffed. "They never last."

"I did."

"Well you're a very special boy."

"Don't let Emma hear you say that."

"Or your boyfriend?" he said, grinning as he nodded towards the door.

I turned around, startled. Dominic had just walked into the café. He saw me, waved, and then went and sat at a table by the window.

"Don't hang out for too long. We're busy," Klyde said. "And try not to get too mushy. This is a family place."

"Tell that to the shelf in the back that you and Emma have banged into oblivion," I said.

I bent down and checked out the deserts behind the counter before selecting a piece of cheesecake. I slid it onto a tray with a couple of coffees, making sure to dump a handful of sugar packs next to the one of the mugs.

Klyde raised his eyebrows. "That'll be eight bucks."

"I'll pay for it later with my winning smile."

"I can't use that for my mortgage," he said resentfully as I made my way across the room towards Dominic's table.

"Here you go, sir," I said, setting the tray down in front of him.

"There's been a mistake," he said. "I ordered a pretty barista with a sassy mouth."

I slid into the chair across from him, grinning. "What're you doing here anyway? Everything okay?"

"Yup. I just missed you."

"But you saw me this morning."

"Sure, but you left in such a hurry. I wanted to make sure you were really going to work and not running off into the arms of some gorgeous man."

"I'm only interested in the arms of one gorgeous man, thank you very much."

"Just his arms?"

"Well, various parts of him." My grin widened, and then I looked around and said with some surprise: "This is the table where I served you for the first time."

"I remember." He smiled. "I wanted to sit near the window because it was such a nice day, though it didn't end up being half as nice as the view I got in here." He wiggled his eyebrows.

I sliced off the tip of the cheesecake with a fork and held it up. He opened his mouth obediently. As I slipped the cake between his lips, I said casually: "I thought you were high."

He choked a little as he laughed. "What? Why?"

"Because you kept staring at me."

"That was your fault. You have a very distracting face." He leaned forward and tapped his mouth. I obediently fed him another bite of cake. Our knees touched under the table. "What else did you think about me?" he asked, his eyes wandering across my face.

"I thought a guy who would go to town on a piece of cheesecake in front of God and everyone was a total freak. You see how we're using this fork? This is how cake is actually supposed to be eaten."

He licked his lips and smiled. "This piece is just as good as the last one…though I've had the pleasure of licking much sweeter treats since then."

"There are children around, sir."

"That's their parents' problem." He inched forward until our fingers interlaced on top of the table. His voice grew softer. "I love you, Theodore."

I stared down at our hands, blinking hard, and then I summoned the courage to meet his eyes.

"Me too."

We sat like that for a bit, holding each other's gaze across the table while the space around us filled with the smell of freshly ground coffee and the bustle of happy strangers. After a few minutes I realized our hands were resting on top of something sticky. There was some residue on the table, some discarded syrup, maybe, that hadn't been wiped off yet. It had transferred to my knuckle, and it glistened wetly in the sun. Dominic followed my gaze.

"Do you need to run to the bathroom?" He started to release my hand, but I tightened my grip and pulled him closer.

"Later."

The branches on the trees outside the café were starting to swell with little green buds. It was cold sitting by the window. But Dominic's hand was hot, and the steam rising from the coffee mugs between us filled the space with warmth.